"Is this what you are looking for, Colonel Mallory?" Raoul Guyon said softly.

Mallory got to his feet and turned. Guyon stood on the other side of the table, a drawer open, holding the small electronic transmitter that was Mallory's only link with the department.

"Good man," Mallory said, and took a step forward.

Guyon dropped the set to the floor and ground his heel into it twice, at the same time taking the Luger from his coat pocket.

Mallory stood staring at him. Guyon was supposed to be his friend, his colleague. Had he become a traitor?

Suddenly a man stepped out of the shadows of the dark galley, a submachine-gun in his hands. He pointed it at Mallory.

Mallory had not expected this. Mallory had not expected this at all. . . .

WRATH OF THE LION

Jack Higgins

A FAWCETT GOLD MEDAL BOOK

Fawcett Publications, Inc., Greenwich, Connecticut

WRATH OF THE LION

THIS BOOK CONTAINS THE COMPLETE TEXT OF
THE ORIGINAL HARDCOVER EDITION.

A Fawcett Gold Medal Book reprinted by arrangement with
Harold Ober Assoc., Inc.

ISBN 0-449-13739-2

Printed in the United States of America

10 9 8 7 6 5 4 3 2 1

For Joe Cooper—good friend

The wrath of the lion
is the wisdom of God.

WILLIAM BLAKE

Contents

1

●

Storm Warning

THE graticules misted over, momentarily obscured by a curtain of green water, but as the tip of the periscope broke through to the surface the small untidy freighter jumped into focus with astonishing clarity. Lieutenant Fenelon gripped the handles of the eyepiece and his breath escaped in a long sigh.

Beside him, Jacaud said, "The *Kontoro?*"

Fenelon nodded. "Not more than five hundred yards away."

Jacaud dropped his cigarette and ground it into the deck with his heel. "Let me see."

Fenelon stood back, conscious of the hollowness at the base of his stomach. He was twenty-six years of age and had never seen action, never known what war was like except through the eyes of other men. But this—this was a new sensation. He felt strangely dizzy and passed a hand across his eyes as he waited.

Jacaud grunted and turned. He was a big, dangerous-looking man badly in need of a shave, a jagged scar bisecting his right cheek.

"Nice of them to be on time."

Fenelon took another look. The *Kontoro* moved slowly to the right across the little black lines etched on the glass of the periscope and his throat went dry. He was already beginning to taste a little of that special excitement that takes possession of the hunter when his quarry is in plain sight.

"One torpedo," he said softly. "That's all it would take."

Jacaud was watching him, a strange, sardonic smile on his face. "What would be the point? No one would ever know."

"I suppose not." Fenelon called the control room from his voice-pipe. "Steer one-oh-five and prepare to surface."

He whipped the periscope down, the hiss it made as it slid into its well mingling with the clamour of the alarm klaxon. As he turned, brushing sweat from his eyes, Jacaud took a Lüger from his pocket. He removed the clip, checked it with the rapidity of the expert and slammed it back into the butt with a click that somehow carried with it a harsh finality.

He lit another cigarette. When he looked up he was no longer smiling.

In the wheelhouse of the *Kontoro* Janvier, the first officer, yawned as he bent over the chart. He made a quick calculation and threw down his pencil. By dead reckoning they were forty miles west of Ushant and the weather forecast wasn't good. Winds of gale force reported imminent in sea areas Rockall, Shannon, Sole and Finisterre.

For the moment there was only an unnatural calm, the sea lifting in a great oily swell. Janvier was tired, his eyes gritty from lack of sleep. A native of Provence, he had never managed to get used to the cold of these northern seas and he shivered with distaste as he gazed out into the grey dawn.

Behind him the door to the companionway clicked open and the steward entered holding a steaming cup of coffee in each hand. He gave one to Janvier and the other to the helmsman, taking his place at the wheel for a few moments while the man drank.

Janvier opened the door and walked out on to the

bridge. He stood at the rail drinking his coffee and breathing deeply of the cold morning air, feeling considerably
more cheerful. Once across Biscay there was the long run
south to look forward to—Madeira, then the Cape and
sun all the way. He finished his coffee, emptied the dregs
over the side and started to turn.

A hundred yards to starboard there was a sudden surge
in the oily water. It boiled in a white froth and a submarine broke through to the surface, strange and alien like
some primeval creature in the dawn of time.

Janvier stood at the rail, trapped by surprise. As he
watched, the conning-tower hatch opened and a young
officer in peaked cap appeared, followed by a sailor who
immediately hoisted a small ensign. A sudden gust of
wind lifted it stiffly, the red, white and blue of the tricolour
standing out vividly against the grey clouds.

The steward emerged from the wheelhouse and stood
at the rail. "What do you make of her, sir?"

Janvier shrugged. "God knows. Better get the captain."

A third sailor appeared in the conning tower, a signal-
ling lamp in his hands. The submarine moved in closer,
narrowing the gap, and the lamp started to wink rapidly.

A reserve naval officer, Janvier had no difficulty in
reading the signal for himself. When he had deciphered it
he stood at the rail frowning for a moment, then went into
the wheelhouse and unhooked the signal-lamp.

As he moved back to the rail, the light flickered again
from the conning tower, repeating her request. As Janvier
replied with the "Message received" signal, the captain
came up the ladder from the well-deck, the quartermaster
close behind.

Henri Duclos was nearly fifty, and after thirty years at
sea, five of them as a corvette captain with the Free French
Navy, he found it difficult to be surprised by anything.

"What's all this?" he demanded.

"They've made the same signal twice," Janvier told
him. " 'Heave to. I wish to come aboard.' "

"What have you replied?"

"Message received."

Duclos went into the wheelhouse and came back with

a pair of binoculars. He examined the submarine for a moment and grunted. "She's French all right. I can see the uniforms. Small for a sub, though." He handed the binoculars to the quartermaster. "What do you make of her?"

The old man took his time and then nodded. "*L'Alouette*. I saw her in Oran last year when the fleet was exercising. An ex-U-boat. Experimental job the Germans were working on at the end of the war. One of those the navy took over."

"So now we know who she is," Duclos said. "The point is, what in the hell does she want with us?" He turned to Janvier. "Ask her to be more explicit."

There was a pause while the lamps flickered again, and Janvier turned blankly. "She says: 'Imperative I board you. Matter of national importance. Please observe radio silence.' "

The lamp on the conning tower of the submarine was still. "What shall I reply, sir?" Janvier said.

Duclos raised the binoculars to his eyes for a moment then took them down. "What can you reply? If it's important enough for them to send a blasted sub after us, then it's important. Signal: 'Come aboard.' " He grimaced at the quartermaster. "I was looking forward to all that sun. My rheumatism's been killing me lately. Let's hope we don't have to go into Brest."

The quartermaster shrugged. "Stranger things are happening in the Republic these days."

"Which republic?" Duclos demanded sardonically. "Stand to all hands and get a ladder over the side."

The quartermaster moved away and Janvier lowered the lamp. "They thank us for our co-operation."

"Do they, now?" Duclos observed. "Let's hope they aren't wasting our time. Stop all engines."

Janvier moved into the wheelhouse and Duclos took out his pipe and filled it from a worn leather pouch, watching the submarine as he did so. The forward hatch was opened and a large yellow dinghy hauled out and inflated. As the freighter started to slow, the two vessels drifted together until finally the gap had narrowed to no more than twenty or thirty yards.

The submarine commander climbed down the ladder from the conning tower and paused at the bottom, watching the half-dozen sailors working on the dinghy. He was slim and rather boyish in his reefer jacket and rubber boots, and the peaked cap was tilted rakishly to one side. He glanced up at Duclos, smiled and waved, then walked along the hull and stepped down into the dinghy.

He was followed by half a dozen sailors, most of whom carried sub-machine-guns slung across their backs. Four of them paddled the boat across the narrow strip of water towards the ladder that had been dropped over the side of the *Kontoro*. Two sailors, still standing by the forward hatch of the submarine, carefully paid out a connecting line.

"Carrying a lot of hardware, aren't they?" Janvier said.

Duclos nodded. "I don't like the look of this at all. It could be messy enough to rub off on all of us. Perhaps they're after someone in the crew. An O.A.S. man trying to get out of the country or something like that."

The sailors came over the side quickly. Three of them unslung their sub-machine-guns and stayed in the well-deck and the young officer mounted the ladder to the upper deck, briskly followed by the other three.

He held out his hand and smiled. "Captain Duclos? My name is Fenelon. Sorry about all this, but I'm only obeying orders, you understand."

The man who came up the ladder next had a scarred and brutal face and cropped hair. Like Fenelon, he wore a naval reefer jacket and rubber boots, but no cap. He leaned casually against the rail and lit a cigarette. The other two sailors spaced themselves behind Fenelon, machine-guns ready.

Duclos began to feel distinctly uneasy. "Look, what's going on? What's this all about?"

"All in good time," Fenelon said. "You complied with my request to maintain radio silence?"

"Of course."

"Good." Fenelon turned and nodded briefly to one of the sailors, who crossed the deck to the wireless room which stood at the rear of the wheelhouse, opened the door and went inside.

A cry of alarm was followed by a burst of fire. A moment later the radio operator staggered through the door, blood on his face. He dropped to his knees and Janvier moved quickly to pick him up.

"The radio," the man moaned. "He put a burst through it."

There was a sudden, ugly murmur from the crew in the well-deck that was answered by a volley of firing, bullets hissing through the steel rigging lines. Duclos glanced over the rail and saw that a heavy machine-gun had been mounted on a swivel on the rim of the conning tower. Even allowing for the difference in height between the two vessels, it was still capable of reducing most of the deck area of the *Kontoro* to a bloody shambles.

He turned slowly, his face pale. "Who are you?"

Fenelon smiled. "Exactly what we seem, Captain. The commanding officer and crew of the submarine *L'Alouette*. Under special orders, but serving France, I assure you."

"What do you want?" Duclos said.

"One of your passengers, Pierre Bouvier. I understand he is travelling with you as far as Madeira?"

Duclos's rage, hardly contained, flooded out in a roar of anger. "By God, I'll see you in hell first! I'm still captain of this ship."

Still leaning comfortably against the rail, Jacaud pulled the Lüger from his pocket and shot him neatly through the left leg. Duclos screamed as the heavy slug splintered his knee-cap and rolled over on the deck, face twisted in agony.

"To encourage the rest of you," Jacaud said calmly. "Now get Bouvier up here."

As Janvier turned, a quiet voice said: "No need, monsieur. He is here."

The man who stepped out of the saloon companionway was well past middle age. Tall and thin with stooping shoulders, he had the angular bony face of the ascetic and thinning grey hair. He wore a raincoat over pyjamas and a small, grey-haired woman clutched his arm fearfully. Behind them, two other passengers, clothes hastily pulled on, hesitated in the doorway.

"You are Pierre Bouvier?" Fenelon demanded.

"That is correct."

Jacaud nodded to one of the sailors. "Bring him over here."

The woman's voice lifted at once, but Bouvier quietened her and allowed himself to be led forward. The sailor placed him with his back to the rail and went and stood beside Jacaud. "What do you want with me?" Bouvier said.

"A month ago at Fort-Neuf you were public prosecutor at a trial," Fenelon said. "A trial at which six good friends of ours received the death sentence."

"So, the O.A.S. is in this?" Bouvier shrugged. "I did my duty as I saw it. No man can do more."

"You will, I am sure, allow us the same privilege, monsieur." Fenelon produced a document from his pocket, unfolded it and read rapidly. " 'Pierre Bouvier, I must inform you that you have been tried in your absence and found guilty of the crime of treason against the Republic by a military tribunal of the Council of National Resistance.' "

He paused and Bouvier cut in gently, "And the sentence of the court is death?"

"Naturally," Fenelon said. "Have you anything to say?"

Bouvier shrugged and an expression of contempt crossed his face. "Say? Say what? There is no charge to answer. I know it and you know it. Frenchmen everywhere will——"

Jacaud plucked the sub-machine-gun from the hands of the sailor standing next to him, aimed quickly and fired a long burst that drove Bouvier back against the rail. He spun round, the material of his raincoat bursting into flame as bullets hammered across his back, and fell to the deck.

His wife cried his name once, took a single step forward

and fainted, one of the passengers catching her as she fell
backwards.

From the well-deck there was a strange, muted sigh
from the crew and then there was only silence. Jacaud
tossed the machine-gun to the sailor he had taken it from
and went down the ladder without a backward glance.
Fenelon looked as if he might be sick at any moment. He
nodded to his men and hurriedly followed the big man,
missing a step half-way down and almost falling to the
deck.

They went over the side one by one and from the conning tower of the submarine the heavy machine-gun covered them menacingly. When they were all in the dinghy
the sailors standing by the forward hatch hauled on the
line quickly.

They left the dinghy to drift and everyone scrambled
down through the hatch except Fenelon, who walked
along the hull and climbed the ladder to the conning
tower. He stood looking up at the freighter for a moment
as the two vessels drifted apart, and on the *Kontoro* there
was a strange, uncanny silence.

The two sailors dismounted the machine-gun and disappeared. Fenelon remained only a moment or two longer
before following. The conning-tower hatch clanged shut,
the sound echoing flatly across the water.

On the *Kontoro* it was as if a spell had been broken and
everyone surged forward to the rail. Janvier had never
felt quite so helpless in his life before and for some unaccountable reason was strangely close to tears.

In the distance the wind was already beginning to lift
the waves into whitecaps and he remembered the gale
warning. *L'Alouette* sank beneath the waves like a grey
ghost, the tricolour waved bravely, then that too disappeared and there was only the sea.

2

●

To Sup with the Devil

A THIN sea fog rolled in from Southampton Water as the taxi turned the corner and pulled in to the kerb. Anne Grant peered out through the window at the dim bulk of the building rearing into the night.

The original structure had been Georgian, so much was obvious, but the years had left their mark. A line of uneven steps lifted to the door, the paint cracked and peeling in the diffused yellow light of a street-lamp. Above it a small glass sign said *Regent Hotel*.

She tapped on the partition and the driver opened it. "Are you sure this is the place?"

"Regent Hotel, Farthing Lane. That's what you said and that's where I've brought you," the man replied. "It's only a doss-house, lady. The sort of place sailors come to for a kip on their first night ashore. What did you expect —the Ritz?"

She opened the door and got out, hesitating for a moment as she gazed up at the damp, crumbling façade of the hotel. Except for the lapping of water against the wharf pilings on the other side of the street, it was completely quiet. When a café door was opened somewhere in the middle distance the music and laughter might have been coming from another planet. She gave the driver ten shillings, told him to wait and went up the steps.

The corridor was dimly lit, a flight of stairs rising into the shadows at the far end. She wrinkled her nose in distaste at the stale smell compounded of cooking odours and urine and moved forward.

There was a door to the left, the legend *Bar* etched in acid on its frosted-glass panel. When she opened it she found herself in a long, narrow room, the far end shrouded in darkness. An old marble-topped bar fronted one wall, a cracked mirror behind it, and a man leaned beside the beer pumps reading a newspaper.

In one corner a drunk sprawled across a table facedown, his breath whistling uneasily through the stillness. Two men sat beside a small coal fire talking softly as they played cards. They turned to look at her and she closed the door and walked past them.

The barman was old and balding, with the sagging, disillusioned face of a man who had got past being surprised at anything. He folded his paper neatly and pushed it under the bar.

"What can I do for you?"

"I'm looking for a Mr. Von Sondergard," she said. "I understand he's staying here."

Beyond the barman the two men by the fire were watching her in the mirror. One of them was small and squat with an untidy black beard. His companion was at least six feet tall with a hard, raw-boned face and hands that never stopped moving, shuffling the cards ceaselessly. He grinned and she returned his gaze calmly for a moment and looked away.

"Sondergard?" the barman said.

"She'll be meaning the Norwegian," the tall man said in a soft Irish voice.

"Oh, that fella?" The barman nodded. "Left yesterday."

He ran a cloth over the surface of the bar and Anne Grant said blankly: "But that isn't possible. I only hired him last week through the seamen's pool. I've a new motor-cruiser waiting at Lulworth now. He's supposed to run her over to the Channel Islands tomorrow."

"You'll have a job catching him," the Irishman cut in. "He shipped out as quartermaster on the *Ben Alpin* this morning. Suez and all points east." He got to his feet and crossed the room slowly. "Anything I can do?"

Before she could reply a voice cut in harshly: "How about some service this end for a change?"

She turned in surprise, realizing for the first time that a man stood in the shadows at the far end of the bar. The collar of his reefer jacket was turned up and a peaked cap shaded a face that was strangely white, the eyes like dark holes.

The barman moved towards him and the Irishman leaned against the bar and grinned at Anne. "How about a drink?"

She shook her head gently, turned and walked to the door. She went out into the corridor and paused at the top of the steps. The taxi had gone and the fog was much thicker now, rolling in across the harbour, swirling round the street-lamps like some living thing.

She went down the steps and started along the pavement. When she reached the first lamp she paused and looked back. The Irishman and his friend were standing in the doorway. As she turned to move on, they came down the steps and moved after her.

Neil Mallory lit another cigarette, raised his whisky up to the light, then set it down. "This glass is dirty."

The barman walked forward, a truculent frown on his face. "And what do you expect me to do about it?"

"Get me another one," Mallory said calmly.

It was some indefinable quality in the voice, a look in the dark eyes, that made the barman swallow his angry retort and force a smile. He filled a fresh glass and pushed it across.

"We aim to please."

"That's what I thought," Mallory said, his eyes following the Irishman and his friend as they went through the door after the woman. He took the whisky down in one easy swallow and went after them.

He stood at the top of the steps listening, but the fog smothered everything, even sound. A ship moved across the water, its fog-horn muted, alien and strange, touching something deep inside him. He shivered involuntarily. It was at that moment that Anne Grant cried out.

He went down the steps and stood listening, head slightly forward. The cry sounded again from the left, curiously flat and muffled by the fog, and he started to run.

He turned the corner on to a wharf at the far end of the street, running silently on rubber-soled feet, and took them by surprise. The two men were holding the struggling woman on the ground in the yellow light of a street-lamp.

As the Irishman turned in alarm, Mallory lifted a foot into his face. The man staggered back with a cry, rolled over the edge of the wharf and fell ten feet into the soft sludge of the mudbank.

The bearded man pulled a knife from his pocket and Mallory backed away. The man grinned and rushed him. As the knife came up, Mallory grabbed for the wrist, twisting the arm up and out to one side, taut as a steel bar. The man screamed like a woman and dropped the knife. Mallory struck him a savage blow across the side of the neck with his forearm and he crumpled to the ground.

Anne Grant leaned against the wall, her face pale in the sickly yellow light, blood streaking one cheek from a deep scratch. She laughed shakily and brushed a tendril of dark hair from her forehead.

"You don't do things by halves, do you?"

"What's the point?" he said.

Her jersey suit was soiled and bedraggled, the blouse ripped to the waist. When she moved forward, she limped heavily on her right foot. She stopped to pick up her hand-bag and the bearded man groaned and rolled on his back.

She looked down at him for a moment, then turned to Mallory. "Are you going to call the police?"

"Do you want me to?"

"Not particularly." She started to shake slightly. "Suddenly it seems colder."

He slipped off his reefer jacket and hung it around her shoulders. "What you need is a drink. We'll go back to the hotel. You can use my room while I get you a taxi."

She nodded down at the bearded man. "Will he be all right?"

"His kind always are."

He took her arm. They walked to the corner and turned into the street. It started to rain, a thin drizzle that beaded the iron railings like silver. There was a dull, aching pain in her ankle and the old houses floated in the fog, unreal and insubstantial, part of the dark dream from which she had yet to awaken, and the pavement seemed to move beneath her feet.

His arm was instantly around her, strong and reassuring, and she turned and smiled into the strange, pale face, the dark eyes. "I'll be all right. A little dizzy, that's all."

The hotel sign swam out of the fog to meet them and they went through the entrance and mounted the rickety stairs. His room was at the end of the corridor and he opened the door, switched on the light and motioned her inside.

"Make yourself at home. I'll be back in a couple of minutes."

The room had that strange, rather dead, atmosphere typical of cheap hotels the world over. There was a strip of worn carpet on the floor, an iron bed, a cheap wardrobe and locker. The one touch of luxury was the washbasin in the corner by the window and she hobbled across to it.

Surprisingly, there was plenty of hot water and she washed her face and hands, then examined herself in the mirror that was screwed to the wall above the basin. The scratch on her cheek was only superficial, but her suit was ruined. Otherwise she seemed to have sustained no real damage. She was sitting on the edge of the bed examining her ankle when he returned.

He placed a half-bottle of brandy and two glasses on

top of the bedside locker and dropped to one knee beside her. "Any damage?"

She shook her head. "A nasty graze, that's all."

He pulled a battered fibre suitcase from under the bed and took out a heavy fisherman's sweater which he dropped into her lap. "You'd better put that on. You're wet through."

When she had pulled it over her head and rolled up the long sleeves, he rested her right foot on his knee and bandaged the damaged ankle expertly with a folded handkerchief. She watched quietly.

He was of medium height, with broad shoulders, and wore the sort of clothes common to sailors. A cheap blue-flannel shirt and heavy working trousers in some dark material, held up by a broad leather belt with a brass buckle. But this was no ordinary man. He had a strange, hard, enigmatic face, the face of a man few would care to trifle with. The skin was clear and bloodless; black, crisp hair in a point to the forehead. The eyes were the strangest feature, so dark that all light died in them.

On the wharf he had been terrible in his anger, competent and deadly, and when he looked up suddenly his dark eyes stared through her like glass. For the first time that night genuine fear moved inside her and then his whole face creased into a smile of quite devastating charm, so great, that he seemed to undergo a complete personality change.

"You look about ten years old in that sweater."

She smiled warmly and held out her hand. "My name is Anne Grant and I'm very grateful to you."

"Mallory," he said. "Neil Mallory."

He touched her hand briefly, opened the brandy, poured a generous measure into one of the glasses and passed it to her. "I got the barman to phone for a taxi. It might be some time before it gets here."

"I'd like to know why the driver who brought me didn't wait," she said. "I asked him to."

"They're not too keen on hanging around the dock area at night. It's a rough place and taxi-drivers are obvious targets." He grinned. "That goes double for good-looking young women, by the way."

She smiled ruefully. "Don't rub it in. I'd no idea what I was letting myself in for, but I was getting desperate. I'd been waiting in Lulworth for someone for most of the day. When it became obvious that he wasn't going to show up I decided to come looking for him."

"Van Sondergard?" Mallory said. "I heard you ask the barman about him."

"Did you know him?"

"He had a room along the corridor from here. I had a drink with him once when he came in the bar. Nothing more than that. Where did you meet him?"

"I didn't," she said. "The whole thing was arranged through the seamen's pool. I told them I need someone to take a motor-cruiser across to the Channel Islands for me and captain her for a month or so until my sister-in-law and I were capable of looking after her ourselves. I also told them we'd prefer someone who'd done a little skin-diving. They put me in touch with Sondergard." She sighed. "He seemed rather keen on the idea. I'd love to know what changed his mind."

"It was very simple really. He was sitting in the bar half drunk, feeling rather sorry for himself, when one of his old captains walked in, due out on the morning tide for Suez and short of a quartermaster. Three drinks was all it took for Sondergard to pack his duffel and go off with him. Sailors have a habit of doing things like that."

He swallowed his brandy, took out an old leather cigarette case and offered her one. "Are you a sailor, Mr. Mallory?" she asked as he struck a match and held it forward in cupped hands.

He shrugged. "Amongst other things. Why?"

"I wasn't sure. If I'd been asked I'd have said you were a soldier."

"What makes you say that?"

"I think you could say I know the breed. My father was one and so was my husband. He was killed in Korea."

There didn't seem anything to say and Mallory lit a

cigarette and walked to the window. He peered outside, then turned.

"The motor-cruiser you mentioned, what kind is it?"

"A thirty-footer by Akerboon. Twin screw, steel hull."

"Only the best?" He looked suitably impressed. "How's she powered?"

"Penta petrol engine. She'll do about twenty-two knots at full stretch."

"Depth-sounder, automatic steering, every latest refinement?" He grinned. "I'd say she must have cost you all of seven thousand pounds."

"Not me," she said. "My father-in-law. All I did was obey orders. He told me exactly what he wanted."

"Sounds like a man who's used to getting his own way."

She smiled. "A habit he finds hard to break. He's a major-general."

"Grant?" Mallory frowned. "Are you talking about Iron Grant? The Western Desert man?"

She nodded. "That's right. He's been living in the Channel Islands since he left the army. I keep house for him."

"What does the old boy do with himself these days?"

"He's almost blind now," she said, "but he's still amazingly active and he's made quite a reputation for himself as a war historian. He uses a tape-recorder and his daughter Fiona and I type up his notes for him."

"You said you wanted Sondergard to have had some experience as a skin-diver? Why was that?"

"It wasn't essential, but he could have been useful. In the fifteenth century a small fishing village and fortress on Île de Roc were inundated. The ruins are now about eight fathoms down a few hundred yards off-shore. We're making a survey. Fiona and I have been doing most of the diving so far."

"Sounds interesting," he said. "You shouldn't find any difficulty in getting another man from the pool to take on a job like that."

As he looked out of the window and down into the yellow fog she said quietly, "I was wondering whether you might be interested?"

He turned slowly, a slight frown on his face. "You don't know anything about me."

"What is there to know? You told me yourself you were a sailor."

"From necessity," he said. "Not choice."

"You couldn't handle *Foxhunter,* you mean?"

"Is that her name? Oh, yes, I've handled boats like that before. I've even done a little skin-diving."

"Eighty pounds a month and all found," she said. "Does that tempt you?"

He grinned reluctantly. "It does indeed, Mrs. Grant."

She held out her hand in a strangely boyish gesture. "I'm glad."

He held it for a moment, looking into her eyes gravely. Her smile faded, and again she was conscious of that vague irrational fear. Something must have shown on her face. Mallory's hand tightened on hers and he smiled gently. In that single moment her fear disappeared and an inexplicable tenderness flooded through her. A horn sounded outside in the street and he helped her to her feet.

"Time to go. Where are you staying?"

"An hotel in the town centre."

"You should cause quite a sensation going through the foyer," he told her as he took her arm and helped her across to the door.

The fog was clearing a little as he handed her into the taxi. She wound down the window and leaned out to him. "I've several things to attend to tomorrow, so I can't get down to Lulworth again until the evening. I'll see you down there."

He nodded. "You could do with a morning in bed."

She smiled wanly in the pale light, but before she could reply the taxi moved away. Mallory stood looking into the fog, listening to the sound of the engine die into the distance, then turned and went up the steps.

When he entered the bar the barman was still reading his newspaper. "Where are they?" Mallory asked.

The man lifted the flap and jerked his thumb at the rear door. "In there."

When Mallory opened the door he found the Irishman sitting at a wooden table beside a coal fire, a basin of hot water in front of him. His clothes were plastered with mud and he was wiping blood from a gash that ran from his ear to the point of his chin. The man with the black beard lay on an old horse-hair sofa, clutching his right arm and moaning softly.

The Irishman lurched to his feet, his eyes wild. "You bastard. What were you trying to do, kill us?"

"I told you to frighten the girl a little, that's all, but you tried to be clever. Anything you got, you asked for." Mallory took several banknotes from his wallet and tossed them on to the table. "That should settle the account."

"Ten quid!" the Irishman cried. "Ten lousy quid! What about Freddy? You've broken his arm."

"No skin off my nose," Mallory said calmly. "Tell him to try the Health Service."

He walked out and the Irishman slumped into his chair again, head swimming. The barman came in and stood looking at him. "How do you feel?"

"Bloody awful. Who is that bastard?"

"Mallory?" The barman shrugged. "I know one thing. He's the coldest fish I've ever met and I've known a few." He looked down at the bearded man and shook his head. "Freddy doesn't look too good. Maybe I should phone for an ambulance?"

"You can do what the hell you like," the Irishman said violently.

The barman moved to the door, shaking his head. "You know what they say. When you sup with the devil you need a long spoon. I reckon you and Freddy got a little too close."

He sighed heavily and disappeared into the bar.

3

●

London Confidential

THE ROOM was half in shadow, the only light the shaded lamp on the desk. The man who sat sideways in the swivel chair, gazing out through the broad window at the glittering lights of London, was small, the parchment face strangely ageless. It was the face of an extraordinary human being, a man who had known pain and who had succeeded in moving beyond it.

The green intercom on his desk buzzed once and he swung round in the chair and flicked a switch. "Yes?"

"Mr. Ashford is here, Sir Charles."

"Send him in."

The door opened soundlessly and Ashford advanced across the thick carpet, a tall, greying man in his forties with the worried face of the professional civil servant who had spent too much of his life close to the seats of power.

He sat down in the chair opposite, opened his briefcase and produced a file which he placed carefully on the desk. Sir Charles pushed a silver cigarette box across to him.

"What's the verdict?"

"Oh, the P.M. agrees with you entirely. The whole

thing must be investigated. But we don't want the newspapers getting on to it. You'll have to be damn' careful."

"We usually are," Sir Charles said frostily.

"There's just one thing the P.M. isn't too happy about."
Ashford opened the file on the desk. "This fellow Mallory.
Is he really the best man for the job?"

"More than that," Sir Charles said. "He's the best man
I've got and he's worked with the *Deuxième Bureau* before
with some success. In fact, they've asked for him twice.
His mother was French, of course. They like that."

"It's this shocking affair in Perak in 1954 that the P.M.
isn't happy about. Dammit all, the man was lucky to escape prison."

Sir Charles pulled the file across the desk and turned it
round. "This is the record of a quite exceptional officer."
He put on a pair of rimless spectacles and started to read
aloud, selecting items at random. " 'Special Air Service
during the war . . . dropped into France three times . . .
betrayed to the Gestapo . . . survived six months at
Sachsenhausen . . . paratroop captain in Palestine . . .
major in Korea . . . two years in a Chinese prison camp
in Manchuria . . . released 1953 . . . posted to Malaya,
January 1954, on special service.' " He closed the file
and looked up. "A lieutenant-colonel at thirty. Probably
the youngest in the army at that time."

"And kicked-out at thirty-one," Ashford countered.

Sir Charles shrugged. "He was told to clear the last
Communist guerrilla out of Perak and he did it. A little
ruthlessly perhaps, but he did it. His superiors then heaved
a sigh of relief and threw him to the wolves."

"And you were waiting to catch him, I suppose?"

Sir Charles shook his head. "I let him drift for a year.
Bombay, Alexandria, Algiers. I knew where he was. When
I was satisfied that the iron was finally in his soul I
pulled him in. He's worked for me ever since."

Ashford sighed and got to his feet. "Have it your own
way, but if anything goes wrong . . ."

Sir Charles smiled softly. "I know, I end up like Neil
Mallory. Out on my ear."

Ashford flushed, turned and crossed the room quickly. The door closed behind him and Sir Charles sat there thinking about it all. After a while he flicked a switch on the intercom.

"Send in Mallory."

He lit a cigarette and stood by the window, gazing out over the city, still the greatest in the world, whatever anyone tried to say. When he opened the window he could smell the river and the sound from a ship's hooter drifted faintly on the quiet air as it moved down from the Pool.

He was tired and there was a slight ache somewhere behind his right eye. Something he should really see his doctor about. On the other hand, perhaps it was better not to know? He wondered whether Mallory would survive long enough to ever take his place behind the desk in this quiet room. It would have been a comforting thought, but he knew it was rather unlikely.

The door clicked open behind him and closed again. When he turned Mallory was standing beside the desk. An easy-fitting suit of dark worsted outlined his broad shoulders and in the diffused white light his aquiline face gave an impression of strength and breeding, not out of place anywhere.

Sir Charles moved back to his chair and sat down. "How are you, Neil?"

"Pretty fit, sir. I've just had six weeks on the island."

"I know. How's your shoulder?"

"No more trouble. They've done a good job."

Sir Charles nodded. "You'll have to be a little more careful next time, won't you?" He opened a file, took out a typewritten document and pushed it across. "Have a look at that."

He occupied himself with some other papers and Mallory skimmed through the three closely typed sheets of foolscap. When he had finished he handed them back, face expressionless.

"Where's the *Kontoro* now?"

"The destroyer which found her took her straight into

Brest. For the time being the French are holding the lid down tight. Complete security and so on. They can't keep it quiet for more than three or four days. These things always leak out sooner or later."

"What are they trying to do about it?"

"The usual round-up of anyone who's even remotely suspected of being connected with the O.A.S. or C.N.R. On top of that, the *Deuxième Bureau* and the *Brigade Criminelle,* backed by every available military security agent, have been given one order. Find that submarine."

"I shouldn't have thought that would be too difficult."

"I'm not so sure," Sir Charles said. "For one thing this is no ordinary submarine. She's quite small. A thing the Germans were working on at the end of the war."

"What's her radius?"

"Not much over a thousand."

"Which means she could be based in Spain or even Portugal?"

"The French are working along those lines right now, but they've got to be careful. On top of that, they're combing the entire Biscay coast, every creek, every island." He sighed heavily. "I've a horrible feeling that they're completely wasting their time."

"I wondered when you were coming to that," Mallory said.

Sir Charles grinned impishly like a schoolboy, opened a drawer and took out a map which he unfolded across the desk. It was a large-scale Admiralty chart of the Channel Islands and the Golfe de St. Malo.

"Ever hear of Philippe de Beaumont?"

"The paratroop colonel? The one who helped bring de Gaulle back to power?"

"That's right. He was one of the leaders of the military coup of May 1958 and a member of the original Committee of Public Safety. Philippe, Comte de Beaumont. Last survivor of one of the greatest of the French military families."

"And he's living in the Channel Islands?"

"He was the great advocate of a French Algeria. When de Gaulle came down on the side of independence he resigned his commission and left France." Sir Charles drew a circle on the chart about thirty miles south-west of Guernsey. "There's an island called Île de Roc owned by old Hamish Grant."

"You mean Iron Grant, the Western Desert general?"

"That's right. Been living there for five years with his daughter Fiona, writing up the war. His daughter-in-law Mrs. Anne Grant seems to run things. Her husband was killed in Korea. About a mile west of Île de Roc there's a smaller island called St. Pierre."

"And de Beaumont's living there?"

"He bought it from Grant two years ago. There's a sort of castle up on top of the rock, one of those mock-Gothic jobs some crank built during the nineteenth century."

"And you think he's up to no good?"

"Let's put it this way. The French have checked on him for two years now and can't find even the hint of a connection with either the O.A.S. or C.N.R., although he's known to be sympathetic to their aims. Frankly, even their Foreign Office think he's simply a *grand seigneur* who won't come home because he's annoyed with the General."

"And you don't agree?"

"I might have done until yesterday evening."

"What happened to change your mind?"

"I've had a man keeping an eye on de Beaumont for a year now, just as a precaution. There's a small hotel on Île de Roc. He was working there as barman. He went missing Tuesday. Yesterday evening he drifted in on the evening tide. The police went over from Guernsey and picked up the body. Needless to say there isn't even a hint of foul play."

"You think he may have seen something?" Sir Charles shrugged. "I don't see why not. *L'Alouette* left Brest on a routine training patrol two days ago. She could have called at St. Pierre and our man could have seen her. It's pretty obvious that he came across something, and the *Deuxième* agree with me. They're sending a man across to work with you on this thing."

"I wondered when we were coming to that," Mallory said.

Sir Charles pushed a file across. "Raoul Guyon, aged twenty-nine. He was a captain in a colonial parachute regiment. Went straight to Indo-China from St. Cyr in 1952."

Mallory looked down at the photograph. It showed a young man, slim-hipped and wiry, the sleeves of his camouflaged jacket rolled up to expose sunburnt arms. The calm, sun-blackened face, dark eyes, were shaded by a peaked cap that somehow gave him a strangely sinister, forbidding appearance.

"Why did he leave the army?"

"God knows," Sir Charles said. "I should imagine six years in Algeria was enough for any man. He asked to be placed on unpaid leave and Legrande of the *Deuxième* offered him a job."

"When do I meet him?"

"You don't, for the moment. Apparently, he's quite a talented painter. He's using that as a cover. Should book in at the hotel on Île de Roc sometime tomorrow."

"What about me?"

"A little more complicated, I'm afraid. If de Beaumont *is* up to no good, then he'll be expecting company. We need to make your background convincing enough to fool him for at least a day or two, and I might as well tell you now that's all the time we can allow."

"What do I do?" Mallory asked.

Sir Charles opened another file and passed a photo across. The girl who stared out at Mallory was somewhere in her twenties, dark hair close-cropped like a young boy's, almond-shaped eyes slanting across high cheekbones. She was not beautiful in any conventional sense and yet in a crowd she would have stood out.

"Anne Grant?" he said instinctively.

Sir Charles nodded. "She came over this morning to finalize the purchase of a thirty-foot motor-cruiser called *Foxhunter*. It's moored at Lulworth now. Apparently, she hired a seaman through the pool to skipper the thing for a couple of months till she and her sister-in-law get used to it for themselves. A big boat for a couple of girls."

Mallory nodded. "I ran one in and out of Tangiers for a while back in '59. Remember?"

"Think you could handle one again?"

Mallory grinned. "I don't see why not."

Sir Charles nodded in satisfaction. "First you'll have to get rid of this seaman. After that all you have to do is make sure you get his job."

"That shouldn't prove too difficult." Mallory hesitated and went on: "Couldn't we work something out with General Grant? Let him know what we're after? He'd be certain to co-operate."

Sir Charles shook his head. "Before you knew where you were he'd be running the whole damned show. In any case, I'm never happy about bringing amateurs into these things if it can be avoided. They give the game away too easily. Use him by all means, but only in an extreme situation where there's no other way." He got to his feet abruptly. "I want results on this one, Neil; and I want them fast. Cut any corners you have to. I'll back you all the way."

One corner of Mallory's mouth twitched ironically. "I seem to remember someone saying that to me once before."

Sir Charles's face was grave and dispassionate, the eyes calm, and Mallory knew beyond a shadow of a doubt that if necessary the old man would not have the slightest compunction in throwing him to the wolves.

"I'm sorry, Neil," he said.

"At least I know where I stand with you." Mallory shrugged. "That's something."

Sir Charles took an old gold watch from his pocket and checked it quickly. "You'll have to get moving. I've arranged for you to be fully briefed by G3 at eight o'clock. They'll give you everything. Money, seaman's papers and a special transmitter. Report your arrival. After that, radio silence till you have some news. I've arranged for three M.T.B.s to proceed to Jersey, ostensibly for shallow-water exercises. The moment we get anything positive from you they'll move in so fast de Beaumont won't know what's hit him."

Mallory walked to the door. As he opened it, the old man said: "Good luck, Neil. With the right kind this could turn out to be a pretty straightforward one."

"Aren't they all?" Mallory said dryly, and the door closed gently behind him.

4

●

G3

PROFESSOR Yoshiyama was little more than five feet in height and wore a judo jacket and trousers many times washed, a black belt around his waist. The face was the man's most outstanding feature, the skin the colour of parchment and almost transparent. There was nothing weak there. Only strength and intelligence and a kind of gentleness. It could have been that of a saint or scholar. It was, in fact, the face of a great master who had practised his art for more than fifty years.

His voice was dry and rather pedantic, the vowels clipped slightly, but the dozen men sitting cross-legged on the floor were giving him all their attention. High in the balcony of the gymnasium, Mallory leaned on the rail and watched.

"The literal meaning of the two Japanese characters which make up the word *karate* is empty hands," Yoshiyama said. "This refers to the fact that *karate* developed as a system of self-defence relying solely on unarmed techniques. The system was first developed centuries ago on the island of Okinawa during a time when the inhabitants were forbidden to carry arms on pain of death."

There was a strangely old-fashioned flavour to everything he said, as if he were repeating a lesson painfully learned. He turned to a large wall chart which carried an outline of a human figure with all vital points, and their respective striking areas, clearly marked.

"The system consists of techniques of blocking or deflecting an attack and of counter-attacking by punching, striking or kicking." He turned, his face bland, expressionless. "But there is more to *karate* than well-practised tricks and physical force." He tapped his head. "There is also the mental application. You will be taught how to focus all your strength and energy on a single target at any given time. Let me show you what I mean."

He nodded briefly and his two assistants picked up three lengths of planking. They were perhaps two feet long, each plank an inch thick. The two men took up their positions in front of Yoshiyama, holding the three planks between them and slightly above waist-level. In a single incredibly fluid motion the old man's left foot stamped forward and his right fist moved up from the waist, knuckles extended. There was a report like a gunshot and the planks split from end to end.

A quick murmur rose from the class and Yoshiyama turned, quite unperturbed. "It is also possible to snap a brick in half with the edge of the hand." He permitted himself one brief smile. "But this requires practice. Major Adams, please."

A small, wiry, middle-aged man with greying hair and a black patch over his right eye stood up at the back of the class and came forward. Like Yoshiyama, he wore a black belt, but where his left arm should have been a metal limb dangled.

"You will observe that Major Adams is rather a small man," Yoshiyama said. "He is also no longer in the prime of life. If we add to this the fact that he has only one arm one would not under normal circumstances give him much hope of surviving any kind of physical assault. As it happens, however, his circumstances are far from normal."

He nodded to one of his assistants and moved out of the way. The assistant, a young, powerfully built Japanese with dark hair, ran to the far side of the gymnasium. He selected a knife from a table which contained an assortment of weapons, turned and ran forward, a blood-curdling cry surging from his throat.

He swerved to one side, came to a dead stop, then moved in quickly, the knife slashing at the Major's face. Adams moved with incredible speed, warding off the attacking arm with an extended knife-hand block. At the same moment he fell diagonally forward to one side and delivered a roundhouse kick to the groin. In what was virtually the same motion he kicked at his opponent's knee-joint with the same foot. The Japanese somersaulted, ended flat on his back, and the foot thudded across his windpipe.

For a moment they lay there and then both men scrambled to their feet grinning widely. "In other circumstances, and had the blows been delivered with full force, my assistant would now be dead," Yoshiyama said simply.

Adams picked up a towel, started to wipe sweat from his face and caught sight of Mallory in the gallery. He nodded briefly, said something to Yoshiyama and moved across to the door. Mallory met him in the corridor outside.

"What are you trying to do, go out in a blaze of glory?"

Adams grinned. "Every so often I get so sick of the sight of that damned desk that I could blow my top. Yoshiyama provides a most efficient safety-valve." He ran a hand over his right hip and winced slightly. "That last fall hurt like hell. I must be getting old."

As they mounted the stairs at the end of the corridor, Mallory thought about Adams. One of the best agents the department had ever had; all the guts in the world and a mind like a steel trap until the night he'd got too close for someone's comfort and they'd tied a Mills bomb to the handle of his hotel bedroom in Cairo.

And now he was a desk man, running G3, the intelligence section that was the pulse-beat of the whole organization. Some people would have said he was lucky, but not Adams.

He opened a door and walked through a small, neat

office. A middle-aged, desiccated-looking spinster with neat grey hair and rimless spectacles sat behind the typewriter. She glanced up, an expression of disapproval on her face, and Adams grinned.

"Don't say it, Milly. Just tell them I'm ready."

He led the way into his own office. Like Sir Charles's, it commanded a fine view of the river, the desk standing by the window. He opened a cupboard, took out a heavy bathrobe and pulled it on.

"Sorry about the delay. I thought Sir Charles would keep you for an hour at least."

"More like fifteen minutes," Mallory said. "He always goes straight to the heart of things with the sticky ones."

"I wouldn't call it that," Adams said. "Interesting more than anything else. Whole thing could be just a storm in a teacup. Let's go into the projection room."

He opened the far door and they descended a few steps into a small hall. There were several rows of comfortable seats and a large screen. The place was quite deserted. They sat down and Mallory offered Adams a cigarette.

"Any gaps in this one?"

Adams exhaled with a sigh of pleasure and shook his head. "I don't think so. Nothing important, anyway. Has the old man told you much?"

"He's outlined the job, told me who the principals are. No more than that."

"Let's get started, then." Adams turned and glanced up at the projection box where a dim light showed. "Ready when you are."

A section of film started to run a few moments later. It showed a submarine entering port slowly, her crew lining the deck.

"To start with, that's what all the fuss is about," Adams said. *"L'Alouette.* Taken at Oran a couple of years ago."

"She looks rather small. There can't be more than a dozen men on deck."

"Originally a German U-boat. Type XXIII. Just over a hundred feet long. Does about twelve kilometres submerged. Crew of sixteen."

"What about armament?"

"Two twenty-one-inch torpedoes in the bow and she doesn't carry spares."

"Doesn't leave much room for mistakes."

Adams nodded. "They never really amounted to anything. This one was built at Deutsches Werft in 1945 and sunk with all hands in the Baltic. She was raised in '46, refitted and handed over to the French."

The film ended and a slide appeared. It showed a young French naval officer, eyes serious beneath the uniform cap, the rather boyish face schooled to gravity.

"Henri Fenelon, full lieutenant. He's her commander. Age twenty-six, unmarried. Born in Nantes. Father still lives there. Runs a small wine-exporting business."

Mallory studied the face for a moment or two. "Looks weak to me. Ever been in action?"

Adams shook his head. "Why do you ask?"

Mallory shrugged. "He looks as if he could crack easily. What's his political background?"

"That's the surprising thing. We can't find any evidence of an O.A.S. connection at all."

"Probably did it for adventure," Mallory said. "He only needed half a dozen men in the crew to agree with him. They could have coerced the rest."

"Sounds feasible," Adams said. "Let's move on."

Various slides followed. There was an Admiralty chart of Île de Roc, with the harbour, the hotel and General Grant's house all clearly marked. St. Pierre was little more than a rock lifting a hundred or so feet out of the sea and crowned by the Victorian Gothic castle.

Mallory shook his head. "God knows how they ever managed to build the damned thing out there."

"Eighteen-sixty-one," Adams said. "A self-made industrialist called Bryant. Bit of a megalomaniac. Saw himself as king of the castle and so on. Cost him better than a hundred thousand to build the place and that was real money in those days."

"I can't see a jetty. Is it on the other side?"

"There's a cave at the base of the cliffs. If you look carefully you can see the entrance. The jetty's inside."

The castle faded and another picture took its place. It

was that of a distinguished-looking man with silvering hair, eyes calm in a sensitive, aquiline face.

"De Beaumont?" Mallory said.

Adams nodded. "Philippe, Comte de Beaumont. One of the oldest of the great French families. He's even a rather distant blood relation of you-know-who, which makes the whole thing even more complicated."

"I know quite a lot about his military history," Mallory said. "After all, he's something of a hero to paratroopers the world over. He came over here during the war and joined de Gaulle, didn't he?"

"That's right. Received just about every decoration possible. Afterwards he went to Indo-China as a colonel of colonial paratroops. The Viets picked him up at the surrender of Dien-Bien-Phu in 1954. After his release he returned to France and was posted to Algeria. He was always at loggerheads with the top brass. Once had an argument with the old man himself at an official reception over what constitutes war in the modern sense."

"That should have been enough to get him put out to grass on its own."

Adams shrugged. "They needed him, I suppose. After all, he *was* the most outstanding paratroop colonel in Algeria at that time. Handled all the dirtier jobs the top brass didn't want to soil its fingers with."

"So he helped bring de Gaulle back to power?"

"That's right. A prime mover in the *Algérie Française* movement. The General, of course, kicked him right in the teeth by granting independence to Algeria after all."

"And de Beaumont cleared out?"

"After Challe's rather abortive little coup last year. Whether or not he was actually mixed up in that little lot we can't be certain. The point is that he left France and bought this place on St. Pierre from Hamish Grant. Caused quite a stir in the French papers at the time."

"And he's kept his nose clean since then?"

"As a whistle." Adams grinned. "Even the French can't turn anything up on him. He runs a boat, by the way. Forty-foot twin-screw motor-yacht named *Fleur de Lys*. The very latest thing for deep-sea cruising with depth-sounder, automatic pilot and 100 h.p. DAF diesels. A bit of a recluse, but he's been seen in St. Helier occasionally. What do you think?"

"I'd say he has the kind of inbred arrogance that can only come from a thousand years of always being right, or at least thinking you were," Mallory said. "Men like him can never sit still. They usually have to be plotting at one thing or another. Comes from that natural assumption that anything conflicting with their own views must be wrong."

"Interesting," Adams said. "He has more the look of a seventeenth-century puritan to me. One of the thin-lipped intolerant variety. A damned good colonel in the New Model Army."

"Jesus and no quarter?" Mallory shook his head. "He's no bigot. Simply a rather arrogant aristocrat with a limited field of vision and an absolute conviction of the rightness of his own actions. When he decides on a plan of attack he follows it through to the bitter end. That's what made him such an outstanding officer. For men like him the rot sets in only if they step outside themselves and see just how much the whole damned thing is costing."

"An interesting analysis, considering you've only seen his photo."

"I know about him as a soldier," Mallory said. "At Dien-Bien-Phu they offered to fly him out. He was too valuable to lose. He refused. In his last message he said they'd been wrong from headquarters staff down to himself. That the whole Dien-Bien-Phu strategy had been a terrible mistake. He said that if his men had to stay and pay the price the least he could do was stay and pay it with them."

"Which probably accounted for his popularity with the troops," Adams said.

"Men like him are never loved by anyone," Mallory said. "Even themselves."

De Beaumont's picture was replaced by another. The face which stared down at them was strong and brutal, the eyes cold, hair close-cropped.

"Paul Jacaud," Adams said. "Aged forty. Parents unknown. He was raised by the madame of a waterfront brothel in Marseilles. Three years in the Resistance, joined the paratroops after the war. He was sergeant-major in de Beaumont's regiment. Medaille Militaire plus a court-martial for murder that failed for lack of evidence."

"And still with his old boss?"

"That's right. You can make what you like out of that. Let's have a look at the angels now."

A picture of Hamish Grant flashed on the screen, a famous one taken in the Ardennes in the winter of '44. Montgomery stood beside him, grinning as they examined a map. He was every inch Iron Grant, great shoulders bulging under a sheepskin coat.

"Quite a man," Mallory said.

"And he hasn't changed much. Of course, his sight isn't too good, but he's still going strong. Written a couple of pretty good campaign histories of the last war."

"What about the family?"

"He's a widower. Son was killed in Korea. At the moment his household consists of his daughter Fiona, daughter-in-law Anne and an ex-Gurkha *naik* called Jagbir who was with him during the war. This is the daughter."

Fiona Grant had long blonde hair and a heart-shaped face that was utterly appealing. "Rather a handful, that one," Adams said. "She was raised in the south of France, which didn't help. They tried Roedean, but that was a complete fiasco. She was finally settled in a Paris finishing school, which apparently suited her. She's at home at the moment."

"I like her," Mallory said. "She's got a good mouth."

"Then see what you think of this one. Anne Grant, the old man's daughter-in-law."

It was the same photograph that Sir Charles had shown him and Mallory stared up at it, his throat for some unaccountable reason going dry. It was as if they had met before and yet he knew that to be impossible. The almond-shaped eyes seemed to come to life, holding his gaze, and he shook his head slightly.

"She's over here now to finalize the purchase of a new boat."

"Sir Charles told me that much. What about this man Sondergard she's hired through the pool?"

"We'll ship him out somewhere. There's no difficulty there. I've already got a little scheme in mind to bring you and Anne Grant together."

They next saw the picture of a Frenchwoman called Juliette Vincente who was working at the hotel on Île de Roc. Nothing was known against her and she seemed quite harmless, as did Owen Morgan, her employer. When the Welshman's face faded away, Mallory straightened in his seat, thinking they had finished. To his surprise another face appeared.

He turned to Adams in surprise. "But this is Raoul Guyon, the man I'm going to work with. I've already seen his picture. What's the idea?"

Adams shrugged. "I'm not sure, but I'm not really happy about the way the French are handling this business. I've got a hunch that old spider Legrande and the *Deuxième* aren't telling us all they could. Under the circumstances it might prove useful to know everything there is to know about Raoul Guyon. He's rather unusual."

Mallory looked again at the photo Sir Charles had shown him. The slim, wiry figure in the camouflage uniform, the sun-blackened face, the calm, expressionless eyes.

"Tell me about him."

"Raoul Guyon, aged twenty-nine. Went straight to Indo-China from St. Cyr in 1952. He's the only known survivor of his particular cadet class for that year, which is enough to set any man apart for a start."

"He wasn't at Dien-Bien-Phu?"

Adams shook his head. "No, but he was at plenty of other hot spots. He was up to his ears in it in Algeria. There was some talk of a girl. Moorish, I think. She was murdered by the F.L.N. and it had a big effect on him. He was badly wounded a day or two later."

There followed a picture of Guyon half raised on a

stretcher, his chest heavily bandaged, blood soaking through. The face was sunken, beyond pain, the eyes stared into an abyss of loneliness.

"There's a lad who's been through the fire," Mallory said.

"And then some. Commander of the Legion of Honour, Croix de la Valeur Militaire and half a dozen mentions in dispatches. On top of that, he paints like an angel."

"A man to be reckoned with."

"And don't you forget it."

For the next twenty minutes they continued to sit there, discussing questions of time and place, some important technical data and various other items, all of which were relevant to the success of the operation. When they finally returned to the office Adams sat behind his desk and nodded at a large and well-filled in-tray.

"Look at that lot," he said with an expression of disgust. "God in heaven, but I'd trade places with you, Neil."

Mallory grinned. "I wonder? Is there anything else?"

Adams shook his head. "Call in at the technical branch. They've got a rather neat line in transmitters for you. They'll give you a call-sign, suitable code and so on. Come back in half an hour. I'll have some identity papers and things ready, plus a rough outline of my little scheme to bring you and Mrs. Grant together."

"Now *that* I look forward to," Mallory said.

And the strange thing was that he really did. As he went along the corridor and descended the stairs to the technical branch the memory of her haunted him. Those strange eyes searching, looking for something.

He sighed heavily. Taking it all in all, it looked as if this whole affair could become really complicated.

5

•

Passage by Night

"FOXHUNTER! Ahoy! Ahoy! *Foxhunter!"*

The boat lay at anchor fifty yards out from the beach, her cream and yellow hull a vivid splash of colour against the white cliffs of the cove. A small wind moved in from the sea, lifting the water across the shingle, and darkness was falling fast.

Anne Grant shivered slightly as a light drizzle drifted across her face. She was tired and hungry and her ankle had started to ache again. She opened her mouth to hail the boat a second time and Neil Mallory appeared on deck. He dropped over the stern into the dinghy and rowed towards her.

He was wearing knee-length rubber boots and when the prow of the fibre-glass dinghy ground on the wet shingle he stepped into the shallows and swung it round so that the stern was beached.

He held out his hand for the girl's suitcase and smiled. "How do you feel?"

"All the better for being here," she said. "It's been a long day. I had a lot of running around to do."

She was wearing a tweed suit with a narrow skirt and

a sheepskin coat. He helped her into the stern seat, pushed off and rowed for the boat.

Anne took in the flared, raking bow and long, sloping deckhouse of *Foxhunter* with a conscious pleasure. As she breathed deeply of the good sea air she smiled at Mallory.

"What do you think of her?"

"Foxhunter?" He nodded. "She's a thoroughbred all right, but that's still an awful lot of boat for two women to handle as a regular thing. How old is your sister-in-law?"

"Fiona is eighteen, whatever that proves. I think you underrate us."

"What about the engines?" he said. "They'll need looking after."

"We've no worries there. Owen Morgan, who runs the hotel on the island, is a retired ship's engineer. He'll give us any help we need and there's always Jagbir."

"Who's he?" Mallory said quickly, remembering that he wasn't supposed to know.

"The General's orderly. He was a *naik* in a Gurkha regiment. They've been together since the early days of the war. He hasn't had what you would call a formal education, but he's still the best cook I've ever come across, and he has an astonishing aptitude for anything mechanical."

"Sounds like a good man to have around the house," Mallory said.

They bumped against the side of *Foxhunter* and he handed her up the short ladder and followed with her suitcase. "What time would you like to leave?"

She took the case from him. "As soon as you like. Have you eaten?"

"Not since noon."

"I'll change and make some supper. We can leave afterwards."

When she had gone Mallory pulled the dinghy round to the stern and hoisted it over the rail. By now darkness was falling fast and he turned on the red and green navigation lights and went below.

He found her working at the stove in the galley, wearing old denims and a polo-necked sweater that somehow made her look more feminine than ever. She looked over her shoulder and smiled.

"Bacon and eggs all right?"

"Suits me," he said.

When it was ready they sat opposite each other at the saloon table and ate in companionable silence. As she poured coffee a sudden flurry of rain drummed against the roof.

She looked up at him, eyebrows raised. "That doesn't sound too good. What's the forecast?"

"Three-to-four wind—rain squalls. Nothing to get worked up about. Are you worried?"

"Not in the slightest." She smiled slightly. "I always like to know what I'm getting into, that's all."

"Don't we all, Mrs. Grant?" He got to his feet. "I think we ought to get started."

When he went on deck the wind had increased, scattering the drizzle in silver cobwebs through the navigation lights. He went into the wheelhouse, pulled on his reefer jacket and spent a couple of minutes looking at the chart.

The door swung open, a flurry of wind lifting the chart like a sail, and Anne Grant appeared at his elbow. She was wearing her sheepskin coat and a scarf was tied around her head, peasant-fashion.

"All set?" he said.

She nodded, her eyes gleaming with excitement in the light from the chart table. He pressed the starter. The engines coughed once asthmatically, then roared into life. He took *Foxhunter* round in a long, sweeping curve and out through the entrance of the cove into the Channel.

The masthead light swung rhythmically from side to side as the swell started to roll beneath them and spray scattered against the window. A couple of points to starboard the red and green navigation lights of a steamer were clearly visible a mile out to sea. Mallory reduced speed to ten knots and they ploughed forward into the darkness, the sound of the engines a muted throbbing on the night air.

He grinned at her. "Nothing much wrong there. With any kind of luck we should have a clear run."

"When do you want me to take over?"

He shrugged. "No rush. Get some sleep. I'll call you when I feel tired."

The door banged behind her and a small trapped wind whistled round the wheelhouse and died in a corner. He pulled the hinged seat down from the wall, lit a cigarette and settled back comfortably, watching the foam curl along the prow.

This was the sort of thing he looked forward to on a voyage. To be alone with the sea and the night. The world outside retreated steadily as *Foxhunter* moved into the darkness and he started to work his way methodically through his briefing from beginning to end, considering each point carefully before moving on to another.

It was in recalling that de Beaumont had been in Indo-China that he remembered that Raoul Guyon had been there also. Mallory frowned and lit another cigarette. There might be a connection, although Adams hadn't said anything about such a possibility. On the other hand, Guyon hadn't been a Viet prisoner, which made a difference. One hell of a difference.

He checked the course, altering it a point to starboard, and settled back again in the seat, turning the collar of his reefer jacket up around his face. Gradually his mind wandered away on old forgotten paths and he thought of people he had known, incidents which had happened, good and bad, with a sort of measured sadness. His life seemed to be like a dark sea rolling towards the edge of the world, hurrying him to nowhere.

He checked his watch, and found, with a sense of surprise, that it was after midnight. The door opened softly, coinciding with a spatter of rain on the window, and Anne Grant came in carrying a tray.

"You promised to call me," she said reproachfully. "I couldn't believe my eyes when I wakened and saw the time. You've been up here a good four hours."

"I feel fine," he said. "Could go on all night."

She placed the tray on the chart table and filled two

mugs from a covered pot. "I've made tea. You didn't seem to care for the coffee at supper."

"Is there anything you don't notice?" he demanded.

She handed him a mug and smiled in the dim light. "The soldier's drink."

"What are you after?" he said. "The gory details?"

She pulled down the other seat and handed him a sandwich. "Only what you want to tell me."

He considered the point and knew that, as always, a partial truth was better than a direct lie. "I was kicked out in 1954."

"Go on," she said.

"My pay didn't stretch far enough." He shrugged. "You know how it is. I was in charge of a messing account and borrowed some cash to tide me over. Unfortunately the auditors arrived early that month. They usually do in cases like mine."

"I don't believe you," she said deliberately.

"Suit yourself." He got to his feet and stretched. "She's on automatic pilot, so you'll be all right for a while. I'll be up at quarter to four to change course."

She sat there looking at him without speaking, her eyes very large in the half-light, and he turned, opened the door and left her there.

He went down to the cabin and flopped on his bunk, staring up at the bulkhead through the darkness. There had been women before, there always were, but only to satisfy a need, never to get close to. That had been the way for a long time and he had been content. Now this strange, quiet girl with her cropped hair had come into his life and quietly refused to be pushed aside. His last conscious thought was of her face glowing in the darkness, and she was smiling at him.

He was not aware of having slept, only of being awake and looking at his watch and realizing with a sense of shock that it was half-three. He pulled on his jacket and went on deck.

There was quite a sea running and cold rain stung his face as he walked along the heaving deck and opened the glass-panelled door of the wheelhouse. Anne Grant was standing at the wheel, her face disembodied in the compass light.

"How are things going?" he asked.

"I'm enjoying myself. There's been a sea running for about half an hour now."

He glanced out of the window. "Likely to get worse before it gets better. I'll take over."

She made way for him, her soft body pressing against his as they squeezed past each other. "I don't think I could sleep now even if I wanted to."

He grinned. "Make some more tea, then, and come back. Things might get interesting."

He increased speed a little, racing the heavy weather that threatened from the east, and after a while she returned with the tea. The wheel kicked like a living thing in his hands and he strained his eyes into the grey waste of the morning.

The sea grew rougher, waves rocking *Foxhunter* from side to side, and again Mallory increased speed until the prow seemed to lift clean out of the water each time a wave rolled beneath them.

Half an hour later they raised Alderney and he became aware of that great tidal surge that drives in through the Channel Islands, raising the level of the water in the Golfe de St. Malo by as much as thirty feet.

He altered course for Guernsey and asked Anne to get the forecast on the radio in the saloon. She took her time over it and when she came back she carried more tea and sandwiches on a tray.

"It's pretty hopeful," she said. "Wind moderating, rain squalls dying away."

"Anything else?"

"Some fog patches in the islands, but nothing to worry about."

Gradually the wind died, the sea calmed and they ran into a clear September morning with a slight mist rising from the water. Mallory opened a window and inhaled the freshness. When he turned she was smiling at him.

"You can handle a boat, Mr. Mallory. I'll say that for you."

"Don't forget to mention the fact in my reference."

She smiled, picked up the tray and went out again. He leaned over the chart and checked the course. *Foxhunter* rounded Les Hanois lighthouse on the western tip of Guernsey an hour and a half later and seagulls and cormorants cried harshly in the sky, sweeping in across the deck from the great cliffs.

Already visibility was becoming worse, fog drifting in patches across the open sea as Guernsey dropped behind the horizon. He set the automatic pilot, leaned over the chart and Anne Grant came in.

"How are we doing?"

"With any kind of luck we should reach Île de Roc in an hour to an hour and a half. Depends on the fog. If we run into any really bad patches things could get tricky."

"There's a large-scale Admiralty chart of the island and its approaches in the top drawer," she said. "I bought it specially."

He took it out and they leaned over it together. Île de Roc was perhaps two miles long and three across, the only anchorage a bay at the southern end. The entire area was encircled by a network of sunken reefs with only two deep-water channels giving anything like a safe passage through.

"I'll take her if you like," Anne said. "I know these waters like the back of my hand and you need to."

"The damned place looks like a death-trap." Mallory shook his head. "I wouldn't like to be drifting in on those shores on a dirty night."

"A lot of good ships have done just that. You see St. Pierre a mile to the north? In the old days whenever a gale was blowing in from the Atlantic ships were often swept between the two islands to founder on the great sunken reef which links them. At low tide the water-level drops as much as thirty feet and you can see some of those old wrecks."

"Dangerous waters to go swimming in."

She nodded. "Especially at the wrong time. As a matter

of fact, the barman from Owen Morgan's hotel was drowned only the other day. His body drifted in the evening before I left."

"Not so good." Mallory moved on quickly. "I see there's a castle marked on St. Pierre."

"A Gothic mausoleum. It's out on a twenty-year lease to a French count, Philippe de Beaumont."

"The place is going to be busier than I thought."

She shook her head. "We don't see much of him. He stays pretty close to home and we don't get many visitors on the island. The hotel only has six bedrooms. They're booked right through the summer, of course, but Owen usually ends the season at the beginning of September. He likes to enjoy the last of the good weather himself."

"He won't need much staff, then?"

"Only during the season and then he uses Guernsey girls. He's had a French cook living in full-time for nearly a year now. She should have left at the end of the season, but stayed on."

"Sounds a rather obvious set-up."

She shrugged. "It's their own affair and she's a nice girl. I hope he marries her."

The fog lifted a little and on either hand the sea broke in a white foam over great reefs. Mallory smiled grimly. "I think this is where you start doing your stuff."

She took over the wheel and altered course half a point. A moment later, through a sudden break in the fog, the towering cliffs of the island loomed into view and then the grey curtain dropped into place again.

Mallory reduced speed and Anne Grant took the cruiser forward into the fog. She seemed completely unperturbed and he shrugged fatalistically, pulled down the other seat and took out a cigarette.

At that moment the whole boat rocked violently and Mallory and the girl were thrown across to the other side of the wheelhouse. *Foxhunter* yawed alarmingly and Mallory shoved the girl away and scrambled across to the spinning wheel.

As he pulled the boat back on course, Anne Grant moved beside him and they peered out into the fog. Perhaps a hundred feet to starboard he caught a glimpse of something solid moving through the water and a sizable wave rolled back to rock *Foxhunter* again.

"And what in the hell was that?" he said.

"Probably a basking shark. They're common enough in these waters, but it must have been a big one to leave a wake like that."

Mallory stared out into the fog, a frown on his face, remembering the force of that wave. Could a shark, however big it was, have set up such a disturbance? He was still thinking about it when they emerged from the last patch of fog and Île de Roc reared out of the sea a quarter of a mile away.

To the west was St. Pierre, much smaller, a little blurred because visibility at that distance still wasn't good. Between the two islands the sea frothed and roared over the great underwater bridge.

"We're in the clear now," Anne Grant said, and he gave *Foxhunter* everything she had as they roared through the water towards the great round cove which opened to meet them.

The water was a deep translucent blue, reminding him strangely of the Mediterranean. A stone jetty jutted fifty feet out from the shore and above it was the hotel, a two-storeyed, white-painted building sheltering in a hollow from the winter gales.

A fifteen-foot launch was moored on the far side of the cove. A young, dark-haired man in sun-glasses was sitting in the stern looking over the side. As he turned towards them a swimmer surfaced and Mallory caught a flash of blonde hair.

When they were a hundred feet from the jetty he cut the engines and *Foxhunter* settled back into the water, drifting in on her own momentum. Anne Grant was already getting the fenders over the side and Mallory ran out to help her. The moment they touched he jumped for the jetty with a line and ran it twice around an iron bollard. *Foxhunter* jerked once, bumped against the jetty and was still.

As he moved to fasten the other line, an engine roared

into life, the sound echoing harshly from the cliffs, and the launch came towards the jetty. The swimmer was already almost there. Anne Grant moved to the port rail and Mallory joined her.

"Fiona," she said simply.

As the girl arrived Mallory leaned down and hauled her up and over the rail. She crouched on deck for a moment, laughing and shaking herself like a young puppy.

"But it's marvellous, Anne. Simply marvellous."

She didn't even look eighteen, long blonde hair trailing damply to her shoulders. She wore a pair of bathing pants and the upper half of a rubber diving suit in bright yellow that fitted her slim figure like a second skin.

She examined Mallory with interest and her eyes widened in approval. "And where did you find *him?*"

Anne laughed and kissed her affectionately. "Now, don't start, Fiona. This is Neil Mallory. He's going to run the boat for us for a month or two till we get the hang of things."

Fiona Grant pushed a tendril of wet hair out of her eyes and held out her hand. "I don't know about Anne, but speaking for myself I'll try not to learn too fast."

The launch was no more than twenty or thirty feet away now and its occupant cut the engine and it drifted in towards *Foxhunter*.

"Who's this, for goodness' sake?" Anne demanded.

Fiona slipped a wet arm in hers. "A simply marvellous man, Anne. He's French. Staying here for a week or two to paint and do a little skin-diving."

"But I thought Owen closed the hotel last week?"

"He did, but luckily I was on the jetty when he came in. I persuaded Owen to change his mind."

The launch bumped against the side and Mallory caught the thrown line. As he looped it round the rail, the Frenchman vaulted on to the deck. He wore a slim-fitting jersey that left his sunburnt arms bare, and the dark glasses gave him the same slightly sinister and anonymous look the peaked military cap had done in the photo in his file.

Fiona took his arm and turned to face them. "Anne, I'd like you to meet Raoul Guyon," she said.

6

●

Iron Grant

THE ancient, grey-stone house was firmly rooted into a hollow in the hill, great beech trees flanking it on either side. At some time a large glass conservatory had been added, running along the whole length of the building, and a series of shallow steps dropped down to a stone terrace.

From the terrace the cliffs fell a good two hundred feet into a small funnel-shaped inlet that would have made a wonderfully sheltered mooring had it not been for the jagged line of rocks stretching across the entrance.

Anne Grant leaned on the wall, a cool drink in her hand, and looked out to sea. It had turned into a beautiful day, surprisingly warm for September, with a scattering of white clouds trailing to the horizon. She felt completely relaxed and at peace, happy to be home again. A foot crunched on gravel. When she turned, her father-in-law stood at the top of the steps.

Major-General Hamish Grant, D.S.O., M.C. and bar, had been well named Iron Grant. Six feet four inches in height, with a great breadth of shoulder, his hair was a snow-white mane swept back behind his ears. He wore an old pair of khaki service trousers and a corduroy jacket.

He probed at the top step with his walking stick. "You there, Anne?"

"Here I am, Hamish."

She went up the steps and took his arm and his great, craggy face broke into a warm smile. "Fiona seemed tremendously excited about the new boat, but she was hardly in the house for a moment before she was changed and off out again."

In a corner of the terrace stood a table containing a tray of drinks and shaded by a large striped umbrella. She led him across and he eased his great bulk into a wicker chair.

"She's gone down to the hotel to meet Raoul Guyon, this young French painter who's staying there. She promised to show him some of the island before lunch."

"What about this fellow Mallory?"

"He should be here at any moment. I asked him to pick up the diving equipment. There was no real hurry, but I thought you might like to meet him."

"I certainly would if only to thank him for the way he handled this Southampton affair." He frowned. "Mallory. Neil Mallory. There's something familiar about that name. Irish, of course."

"He certainly doesn't have an accent."

"And you say he was cashiered for cooking the mess books? That certainly doesn't fit in with the sort of man who'd take on a couple of thugs in a back alley."

"That's what I thought. He's a strange man, Hamish. At times there's something almost frightening about him. He's so curiously remote and detached from things. I think you'll like him."

"I'd love to know why they slung him out," the General said. "Mind you, the War Office, God bless 'em, do some pretty daft things these days."

"I'd rather you didn't raise the subject," she said. "Promise?"

He frowned for a moment and then shrugged. "I don't see why not. After all, a man's past is his own affair. Can he sail the boat, that's the main thing?"

She nodded. "Perfectly."

"Then what have we got to grumble about?" He squeezed her hand. "Get me a brandy and soda like a good girl and tell me some more about *Foxhunter*."

She didn't get the chance. As she was pouring his drink, Jagbir appeared at the top of the steps, Mallory a yard or two behind him.

The Gurkha was short and squat, no more than five feet tall, and wore a neat, sand-coloured linen jacket. He had the ageless, yellow-brown face of the Asiatic and limped heavily on his left foot, relic of a bad wound received at Cassino.

He spoke good English with the easy familiarity of the old servant. "Mr. Mallory's here, General."

The General sipped a little of his brandy and put the glass down again. "What's on the stove?"

"Curried chicken. When would you like to have it?"

"Any time you like. Serve it out here."

Mallory stood at the top of the steps waiting, cap in hand, and Anne smiled up at him. "Would you care to have lunch with us, Mr. Mallory?"

He shook his head. "It's good of you to offer, but I've already arranged to eat at the hotel."

She dismissed Jagbir with a quick nod, trying to hide her disappointment, and Mallory came down the steps.

"This is Mr. Mallory, General," she said formally.

Hamish Grant turned towards Mallory, his head slightly to one side. "Come a bit closer, man. I don't see very well."

Mallory moved to the table and looked down into the cloudy, opalescent eyes. The General reached out and touched him gently on the chest. "My daughter-in-law tells me you're a good sailor?"

"I hope so," Mallory said.

"What was your last ship?"

"An oil-tanker. S.S. *Pilar*. Tampico to Southampton."

The General turned to Anne. "Did you check his papers?" She shook her head and he looked up at Mallory again. "Let's see them."

Mallory took a wallet from his hip pocket, extracted a folded document and union card and tossed them on the table.

"See when he last paid off and check the union card. There should be a photo."

She checked the documents quickly and nodded. "Paid off S.S. *Pilar,* Southampton, IST September." She smiled as she handed them back. "It isn't a very good photo."

Mallory didn't reply and the General continued: "The terms Mrs. Grant agreed with you, you're quite satisfied with them?"

"Perfectly."

"There'll be a bonus of one hundred pounds for you on top. Some token of my gratitude for the way you handled this Southampton business."

"That won't be necessary, sir," Mallory said coolly.

Blood surged into the General's face in an instant. "By God, sir, if I say it is necessary it *is* necessary. You'll take orders like everyone else."

Mallory adjusted his cap and turned to Anne. "You mentioned some diving equipment you wanted me to take down to the boat?"

She took a hurried glance at the General's purple face and said quickly: "You'll find a station wagon in the courtyard at the rear. Jagbir's already loaded it. I'll be down later this afternoon."

"I'll expect you." Mallory turned to the General. "Anything else, sir?"

"No, damn your eyes!" the General exploded.

A smile tugged at the corner of Mallory's mouth. His hand started upwards in an instinctive salute. He caught himself just in time, glanced once at Anne, turned, and ran lightly up the steps.

The General started to laugh. "Pour me another brandy."

Anne uncorked the bottle and reached for his glass. "Am I right in assuming all that was quite deliberate?"

"Of course," Hamish Grant said, "and I'll add to your mystery, my dear. There goes a man who once was used to command, and high command at that. I didn't spend forty years in the army for nothing."

High on the cliffs on the western side of the island Raoul Guyon and Fiona Grant topped a steep hill and paused. Before them the island seemed to tumble over the cliffs and the great jagged spine which joined them to St. Pierre was visible under the water.

"There," she said, making a sweeping gesture with one hand. "Did I lie to you?"

"You were right," he said. "Absolutely magnificent."

"I'll expect to see you up here with your easel first thing in the morning."

"You'll be disappointed. I always work from preliminary sketches, never from life."

She had moved a few feet away, stooping to pick up a flower, and now she turned quickly. "Fraud."

He took a small sketch-pad and pencil from the pocket of his corduroy jacket and dropped to the ground. "Stay where you are, but look out to sea."

She obeyed him at once. "All right, but this had better be good."

"Don't chatter," he said. "It distracts me."

The sun glinted on her straw-coloured hair and her image blurred so that in that one brief moment of time she might have been a painting by Renoir. She looked incredibly young and innocent and yet the wind from the sea moulded the thin cotton dress to her firm young figure with a disturbing sensuousness.

Guyon grunted and pocketed his pencil. "All right."

She dropped beside him and snatched the pad from his hand. In the same moment her smile died and colour stained her cheeks. Inescapably caught in a few brief strokes of the pencil for all eternity, she stood gazing out to sea, and by some strange genius all that was good in her, all the innocence and longing of youth, were there also.

She looked up at him in wonderment. "It's beautiful."

"But you are," he said calmly. "Has no one ever told you this before?"

"I learned rather early in life that it's dangerous to let them." She smiled ruefully. "Until my mother died four years ago we lived in a villa near St. Tropez. You know it?"

"Extremely well."

"In St. Tropez, in season, anything female is in demand and fourteen-year-old girls seem to have a strong appeal for some men."

"So I've heard," he said gravely.

"Yes, life had its difficulties, but then the General bought this little island and I went to school for a couple of years. I didn't like that at all."

"What did you do, run away?"

She pushed her long hair back from her face and laughed. "Persuaded the General to send me to a finishing school in Paris. Now *that* was really something."

Guyon grinned and lit a cigarette. "Tell me, why do you always call him General?"

She shrugged. "Everyone does—except for Anne, of course. She's special. When she married my brother Angus she was only my age. He was killed in Korea."

She paused, a few wild flowers held to her face as she stared pensively into the past, and Guyon lay back, gazing up at the sky, sadness sweeping through him as he remembered another time, another girl.

Algiers, 1958. After five months chasing *fellaghas* in the cork forests of the Grande Kabylie he had found himself in that city of fear, leading his men through the narrow streets of the Kasbah and Bab el Qued, locked in the life-or-death struggle that was the Battle of Algiers.

And then Nerida had come into his life, a young Moorish girl fleeing from a mob after a bomb outrage on the Boulevard du Telemly. He closed his eyes and saw again her dark hair tumbling across a pillow, moonlight streaming through a latticed window. The long nights when they had tried to forget tomorrow.

But the morning had come, the cold grey morning when she had been found on the beach, stripped and defiled, head shaven, body mutilated. The proper ending for a woman who had betrayed her people for a *Frangaoui*. The sniper's bullet of the following day which had sent him back to France on a stretcher had almost carried a welcome oblivion.

Nerida. The scent of her was strong in his nostrils and he reached out and pulled her down, crushing his lips against hers. Her body was soft and yielding and when she swung on to her back her mouth answered sweet as honey. He opened his eyes and Fiona Grant smiled lazily up at him.

"Now what brought that on?"

He leaned on one elbow for a moment and rubbed a hand across his eyes. "Put it down to the sea air. I'm sorry."

"I'm not."

"Then you should be." He pulled her to her feet. "Didn't you tell me you were expected for lunch?"

She held on to his hand. "Come back with me. I'd like you to meet the General."

"Some other time. I've arranged to eat at the hotel."

She turned from him like a hurt child. He restrained a strong impulse to take her in his arms, reminded himself strongly that he had work to do—important work—and walked away. When he reached the top of the rise he hesitated and turned reluctantly.

She was standing where he had left her, head drooping, something touchingly despondent about her. The strong sunlight, streaming through the thin cotton of her dress, outlined her firm young thighs perfectly.

"Damn her!" he said softly to himself. "She might as well have nothing on."

He sighed heavily and went back down the slope.

Mallory lay on his bunk in *Foxhunter* watching the blue smoke from his cigarette twist and swirl in the current from the air-conditioner. He'd had an excellent meal at the hotel in company with Owen Morgan, but there had been no sign of the Frenchman.

His mind went back again to his meeting with Hamish Grant at the house on the cliffs. There had been method behind the old man's bullying, of that he was certain. He had been a soldier himself for too long to subscribe to the opinion that all generals were rather stupid, dull-witted blimps who spent their time either needlessly sending men to their deaths or overindulging at the table.

Behind the worn, leather-coloured face, the half-blind eyes, was a will of iron and a first-rate brain. Iron Grant, who had force-marched his division through the hell that was the Qattara Depression rather than surrender to Rommel, who had led the way down the ramp of the first landing craft to hit Sword Beach on D-Day, was an adversary to be reckoned with by any standards.

And then there was his daughter-in-law. Mallory closed his eyes, trying to picture her face. There was a calmness about her, a sureness that he found disturbing. Even on the wharf at Southampton she had not seemed afraid. It was as if life had done its worst, could do no more. As if nothing could ever really hurt her again. It came to him quite suddenly that she must have loved her husband very much and he was aware of a vague, irrational jealousy.

He heard no sound and yet it was as if a wind had passed over his face and every muscle came alive and singing, ready for instant action. The lower step of the companionway creaked and he reached for the butt of the revolver under his pillow.

"No need, my friend," Raoul Guyon said quietly.

As Mallory opened his eyes, the young Frenchman dropped on to the opposite bunk and produced a packet of cigarettes.

"We missed you at lunch," Mallory said. "What happened?"

Guyon shrugged. "Something came up. You know how it is?"

"I certainly do. There's grass on your jacket."

"A fine day for lying on one's back and contemplating heaven," Guyon said brazenly.

"Not when there's a job to be done." Mallory opened a cupboard under the bunk, took out a bottle of whisky and two glasses and set them on the table. "Business and pleasure don't mix."

"On occasion, I'm happy to say that they do. Am I not supposed to be a fun-loving young artist on vacation?" Guyon poured himself a generous measure of whisky and raised his glass. "*Santé*."

Slim-hipped, lean and sinewy, Raoul Guyon possessed that strange quality to be found in the airborne troops of every country, a kind of arrogant self-sufficiency bred of the hazards of the calling. While unaware of this in himself, he recognized it at once in the Englishman, but there was more than that. Much more. Mallory was the same strange mixture of soldier and monk, of man-of-action and mystic, that he had seen in the great paratroop colonels in Algiers. Men like Philippe de Beaumont. Strange, wild, half-mad fanatics, marred by their experiences in the Viet prison camps, for the time controlling the destiny of a great nation.

But Mallory also had passed through the fire of a Communist prison camp and, like Philippe de Beaumont, he had tried to put into practice those lessons hard learned from his Chinese taskmasters and with the same disastrous result.

Mallory lit a cigarette and leaned back against the bulkhead. "How good is your skin-diving?"

Guyon shrugged. "I know what I'm doing. A little out of practice, that's all."

"Anne Grant wants me to take her out over the reef this afternoon. She's brought a couple of aquamobiles back from the mainland. Wants to try them out. I thought if you asked Fiona nicely you might get yourself invited."

"As a matter of fact, I already have. All part of my business-cum-pleasure activities."

"You don't waste much time." Mallory grinned. "We'll see how things look. We can make a full-scale reconnaissance later tonight."

"You really think there may be something in this business?"

Mallory shrugged. "I wouldn't like to say. As I was bringing the boat in this morning something damned big passed us underwater. Anne Grant said it was a shark. Apparently they're pretty common round here."

"Do you think it's worth reporting?"

Mallory shook his head. "My boss is interested in facts, not possibilities. I've signalled my arrival and nothing more." He opened the cupboard again, took out what was apparently a small transistor radio and held it up. "Amazing what they can do with electronics these days. There are three motor torpedo boats based on St. Helier now, supposed to be on shallow-water exercises. If I give them the word they'll be in here like a shot."

"What's the signal?"

"Their codeword is Leviathan. When we need them we simply signal Code Four. That's all that's needed."

Mallory put the set in a drawer in the table and Guyon helped himself to more whisky. "I was in touch with my own people before I left Guernsey this morning. They've drawn a complete blank where *L'Alouette* is concerned. It's creating something of a situation."

"What in the hell are the O.A.S. trying to prove?" Mallory said. "This sort of thing isn't going to get them anywhere in the long run."

"Desperate men seek desperate remedies. Eight times since 1960 either the O.A.S. or the C.N.R. have conspired to kill de Gaulle. They came closest last month when they ambushed his car on the way to Villacoublay Airport. They picked the leader of that little affair up only last week."

"So this latest business is to prove to people they're still a force to be reckoned with?"

"More than that. That they have a long arm which can reach out to punish those who oppose them. This isn't the first member of the judiciary to be assassinated. At this rate there will soon be no one willing to be connected with the trials of O.A.S. members, especially when to take part carries an automatic death sentence."

"What about Bouvier?"

"He was public prosecutor at a military tribunal which only last month tried six members of the O.A.S. Two were sentenced to death. His execution was stage-managed to have the maximum dramatic effect and the government can't hope to keep it secret beyond the end of the week."

"Which doesn't give us long to handle things here." Mallory frowned. "Have you ever met de Beaumont personally?"

"Only as one of the crowd. He was a member of the original Committee of Public Safety which brought de Gaulle back to power. When it became obvious that the General wouldn't play along with his dream of an integrated Algeria he fell to plotting, or so we think."

"Was anything ever proved against him?"

Guyon shook his head. "It was thought that he was the power behind the scenes in General Challe's abortive coup in 1961, but there was no evidence. Before any could be collected he asked to be placed on unpaid leave and left France. He's extremely wealthy, by the way. One of his uncles married into industry after the first war."

"What does Legrande think about him?"

Guyon laughed. "Legrande has little respect for the aristocracy. He would see the guillotine set up in the old situation and smile at the prospect. He has no proof that de Beaumont is directly connected with the O.A.S., but he is unhappy about him. He would be quite content to see him dead. He has a naturally tidy mind."

"And what's your own opinion?"

"Of de Beaumont?" Guyon hesitated. "He's a dangerous man and no fool. For a year he was in charge of all military intelligence in Algeria, but he was always at loggerheads with the brasshats. He saw war as the Communists see war—as something to be won—and he believed that the end justified the means. Something the *boi-dois* had beaten into him in the Viet camps." Guyon half smiled. "This much at least I would expect you to have in common with him. Legrande told me that you, too, were behind the Communist wire for a time."

"You make him sound interesting," Mallory said. "I'd like to meet him. I've a feeling that would tell me all I need to know."

"Very possibly." Guyon emptied his glass. "Is there anything else you wish me to do?"

"This Frenchwoman who's living at the hotel with

Morgan, Juliette Vincente? In my briefing they said she was harmless. What do you think?"

"Our preliminary report certainly didn't indicate anything unusual. Her mother and father have a small farm in Normandy. One brother, killed doing his military service in Algeria in 1958. She worked at an hotel in St. Malo for six months before coming here."

Mallory nodded. "Sounds all right, but run the usual check on your room, just to make sure it hasn't been searched."

Guyon put on his sun-glasses and got to his feet. "I'll get changed. See you in about half an hour and we'll have a look at that reef." He paused in the doorway and stretched. "It really is a beautiful day. I'm quite looking forward to it."

After he had gone Mallory sat on the edge of the bunk going over things in his mind, trying to work out what might happen, but he knew that he was wasting his time.

If there was one lesson he had learned above all others it was that in this game nothing was certain. Chance ruled every move. He opened one of the lockers, took out the diving gear and started to check it.

7

•

On the Reef

MALLORY vaulted over the rail into the translucent blue water, paused for a moment to adjust the flow of air from his aqualung and swam down in a long sweeping curve that brought him under the hull of *Foxhunter* to where Fiona Grant swayed beside the anchor chain like some exotic flower in her yellow diving suit. A moment later her sister-in-law appeared beside them in a cloud of silver bubbles.

Fiona jack-knifed at once and followed the anchor chain down into the blue mist, her long hair streaming out behind, and Mallory and Anne went after her.

They were perhaps a hundred yards out from the shore on the southern side of the island and the water was saturated with sunlight, so that even when they reached bottom at forty feet visibility was good.

The sea-bed was covered by a great spreading forest of seaweed six or seven feet deep which moved rhythmically with every ebb and flow of current, changing colour like some living thing. Fiona swam into it, fish scattering to avoid her. Mallory paused, hovering over the undulating mass, and Anne tapped him on the shoulder and moved away.

They plunged over a great black spine of rock and a wall complete with arched Norman window loomed out of the shadows a few feet to the right. Anne swam effortlessly through it and Mallory followed.

It was obvious that only the strong tidal currents on this side of the island had prevented the building from being completely silted over centuries before. It had no roof and the walls had crumbled until they stood no higher than four feet above the sand. Beyond, the sea-bed sloped gently into another forest of seaweed, broken walls and jumbled blocks of worked masonry strewn on every side.

Fiona Grant appeared from the gloom and swam towards them. She poised a couple of feet away, put a hand into the nylon bag which was looped to her left wrist and produced a piece of red pottery which she waved triumphantly. Anne raised her thumb and they all turned, swam back across the rocks and struck upwards to *Foxhunter*'s curved hull.

They surfaced by the small ladder suspended over the side, and Anne went up first. Mallory followed her, pulled off his mask and turned to give Fiona a hand. She squatted on the deck, taking the pieces of pottery from her bag one by one and laying them out carefully.

Raoul Guyon had set up an easel next to the wheelhouse and was sketching Hamish Grant, who sat in the bows. The Frenchman put down his pencil and moved across to join them.

The General turned his head sharply. "What's going on?"

"Fiona's found some pottery," Anne said.

Guyon turned to Mallory, a strange, alien-looking figure in his webbed feet and black rubber suit. "What's it like down there?"

"Interesting," Mallory said. "You should try it."

"Perhaps later. I'd like to get my sketches of the General finished and the light is just right."

Fiona unstrapped her aqualung, squatted down on the

deck again and started to sort through the pieces of pottery, completely absorbed by her task.

Anne turned to Mallory. "That's the last we'll see of her today."

"Do you want to go down again?"

She shook her head. "I'd like to try out the aquamobiles. You take one and I'll have the other. We'll go round the point to the St. Pierre reef. I'll show you the Middle Passage and there's at least one interesting wreck."

Guyon helped Mallory bring the two aquamobiles up from the saloon. They were bullet-shaped underwater scooters driven by battery-operated propellers, designed to operate at depths of up to one hundred and fifty feet. They carried their own spotlights for use when visibility was bad.

Anne and Mallory went over the side and Guyon passed down the heavy scooters. Anne moved away at once, running on the surface, and Mallory went after her.

The sea was calm, the sun bright on the face of the water, but as they approached the great finger of rock jutting out into the sea at the western end of the island Mallory became aware of cross-currents tugging at his body. Anne raised an arm in a quick signal and disappeared.

The sensation of speed underwater was extraordinary. To Mallory it seemed as if he were hurtling through space as he chased the yellow-clad figure in front of him and yet his effective speed was not much more than three knots.

The red nose of the scooter whipped through the blue-green water, pulling him across a jumbled mass of black rocks. For a moment currents seemed to pull his body in several directions at once and then he was round the point and into calmer water.

They surfaced by a weed-covered shoulder of rock and Anne sat on its slope half out of the water and pulled up her mask. On either side, and stretching across to St. Pierre, was white water, surf breaking everywhere over the jagged rocks which made up the central reef mass.

"At low tide most of the reef is twenty feet above water," she said. "Stretching all the way to St. Pierre like a giant's causeway."

"Could it be crossed on foot?"

She looked dubious. "I wouldn't like to try. It's only clear for an hour. Something to do with another flood which moves in this way from the Atlantic."

A mile away the great, jagged rock of St. Pierre lifted out of the sea. The castle was perched on the ultimate edge of the cliffs, its strange, pointed Gothic towers in sharp relief against the blue sky. The sea creamed over rocks two hundred feet below.

"What do you think of it?" she said.

"It must have cost a fortune to build even on the golden tide of Victorian prosperity." He shaded his eyes and frowned. "I can't see a jetty."

"It's under the island. If you look carefully beyond the last line of rocks you'll see the entrance in the cliffs. At high water there's only a ten- or twelve-foot clearance."

"Is the water very deep in there?" he said casually.

She nodded. "Even at low water there's a good ten fathoms. There's a fault in the sea-bed which splits the reef along the centre. It runs right under St. Pierre."

"Would that be your famous Middle Passage?"

"That's right, and it's well worth seeing."

She clamped her rubber mouthpiece between her teeth, pulled down the mask and eased herself back into the water. Visibility was still good and Mallory could see the great boulders of the reef four or five fathoms beneath, and then quite suddenly Anne tilted her scooter over a shelf of granite and went down into space.

They moved through a misty tunnel of rock, sunlight slanting through fissures and cracks in the roof in wavering bands of light. In places the passage was reminiscent of a cathedral nave, the rock arched up on either side to support the roof, and then the dimness brightened and they moved into a section which was open to the sea.

Anne was twenty or thirty feet in front and she paused, waiting for him. When he approached she jack-knifed. Mallory went after her, the scarlet nose of his scooter

cleaving the water, fish crowding to either side. At ten
fathoms he moved into a mysterious green dusk with
visibility considerably reduced.

Beneath him she had paused, hovering over a ledge.
When he joined her he saw, to his astonishment, a three-
ton Bedford truck wedged on its side in a large fissure.
The canvas tilt had long since disappeared, but when he
moved in close he saw painted on the side the white star
which all Allied vehicles had carried on D-Day and after.

They moved away again and a moment later the outline of a ship's stern loomed out of the gloom. Every rail,
every line, was festooned with strange submarine growths
and he followed the curving side to where a ragged torpedo
hole gaped darkly at him. Beneath, tilted into a crevasse,
was a Churchill tank, beyond it, the shapes of trucks, a
solitary field-gun's barrel slanting towards the surface.

Mallory followed Anne across the deck to the wheelhouse. The open door swung gently in the current, the
deck around it smashed and broken as if by some internal
explosion. The wheel was still intact and also the compass
in its mounting, encrusted with scales. When Mallory
moved inside he had a strange sensation that someone
should be there, that something was missing. A bad end
for a good ship, he thought, and moved out again. She
tapped him on the shoulder, and together they rose towards
the luminosity that was the surface.

They hauled themselves on to the flat top of a large
rock, dry in the sun, and Anne pulled up her mask and
breathed deeply several times.

"What's the story?" Mallory said.

She shrugged. "One of the D-Day armada that never
made it. She was torpedoed near Guernsey. When her
engines stopped the tide carried her straight in across the
reef. Apparently, the crew got away earlier in the life-
boats."

"Where did you get the story?"

"From Owen Morgan. There are plenty of wrecks in
these waters and Owen knows them all—and their histories. Something of a hobby with him."

"Interesting," Mallory said. "I'd like to take another look. Feel up to it?"

"I don't think so. I'll wait for you here. Don't stay too long. When the tide starts turning there's quite an under-current through the passage."

He was aware of it almost at once like an invisible hand pushing him to one side as he went down over the edge of the reef. The pressure of the water clawed at his mask as the scooter pulled him down and he swerved as a steel mast pierced the gloom.

He hovered over the tilting deck, considering his next move. The sight of the black, gaping entrance to a companionway decided him. He moved inside, switching on the spot which was mounted on top of the scooter.

He moved along the angled corridor and opened the first door he came to. It fell inwards slowly, the room beyond it dark, and he was aware of a strange, irrational fear. He pushed forward boldly, and the light, spreading through the water, showed him a table bolted to the floor, a bunk against one wall and bottles and assorted debris floating against the ceiling.

He swam out and moved further along the corridor to where it disintegrated into a twisted mass of metal, electric wires draped from the roof and, most poignant sight of all, the broken remnants of a human skeleton crushed beneath a girder.

He moved back along the corridor quickly and, the moment he emerged from the companionway, struck up towards the reef. At twenty feet he paused to decompress for several minutes, aware of the current tugging at his body. He surfaced a few yards from the rock and found Anne Grant waist-deep on the edge of the reef, adjusting her equipment.

"We'll have to get moving," she shouted, as he approached and pushed up his mask. "It must be later than I thought. I can feel the tide moving already."

"Is that bad?" he said.

She nodded. "Even the aquamobiles aren't going to do us much good with a five-knot current flowing the other way."

She moved off at once and he went after her. Behind them the entire length of the reef was surging into breakers and he could feel the relentless pressure of the current. He started to flutter-kick with all his strength, and gradually the point grew nearer. Anne turned, gave him a quick wave and they went down.

He could see the weeds on the sea-bed beneath him leaning over on one side, pointing back towards the reef, and the pressure was now a solid wall that he was trying to break through. He kicked again, was dimly aware of the black rocks passing beneath him and then they were round into calm water and his aquamobile seemed to leap forward with a surge of power.

He surfaced and saw Anne at once, over to the right and some distance in front of him. He raised a hand, urging her on, and followed. When he rounded the final point of rock she was perhaps fifty yards in front of him and moving strongly towards *Foxhunter*.

A speedboat was moored beside the ladder, the sunlight gleaming on its scarlet trim, and someone sat in a canvas chair next to General Grant, a tall, distinguished-looking man in dark glasses and linen jacket who stood up and moved to the rail, shading his eyes as Anne approached.

She reached the ladder and he moved to give her a hand. When she climbed up on deck Mallory was still twenty or thirty yards away and he reduced speed.

As he came in under the counter of the speedboat the man who was sitting at the wheel turned to look down at him. He was a large, dangerous-looking individual with a hard face, a jagged scar bisecting the right cheek. Mallory recognized him at once from the photograph he had been shown at his briefing.

He pushed up his mask. "Hello there."

Jacaud looked down at him calmly, nodded, then turned away. Mallory pulled himself to the bottom of the ladder where Raoul Guyon was already waiting, a hand outstretched for the aquamobile.

Mallory went over the rail, squatted on deck and took off his aqualung. Anne Grant was standing a yard or two away, an attractive figure in her yellow diving suit as she talked to the man in the linen jacket.

There was little doubt who he was. The handsome, aristocratic face, the easy poise, spoke of a man who was supremely aware of the fact that God had created the de Beaumonts first.

"Such a nice surprise," she was saying.

"Pure luck that I passed, I assure you. I was trying out my new speedboat." De Beaumont raised her hand to his mouth. "My dear Anne, you grow more delightful each time I see you."

She coloured charmingly and the General cut in: "And now that we've got you you won't get away so easily. You must come to dinner tonight. It's been far too long."

"Please do," Anne said.

He shrugged, still holding her hand. "How can I refuse?"

Raoul Guyon was standing with Fiona beside the deckhouse and Anne turned towards him. "Have you met Monsieur Guyon?"

"I have indeed," de Beaumont said. "I've been looking at these delightful sketches he's done of the General. If he can spare the time perhaps you could persuade him to come across to St. Pierre one day and sketch me?"

"A pleasure," Guyon said.

Anne turned towards Mallory. "And this is Mr. Neil Mallory. He's running the boat for us for a month or two till Fiona and I get used to things."

De Beaumont stood for a moment, looking towards Mallory, and then he slowly removed his sun-glasses. His eyes were a strange, metallic blue and very cold, no warmth in them at all, and yet something moved there, something that instantly put Mallory on the alert.

"Mr. Mallory." De Beaumont held out his hand.

Mallory took it and the grip tightened. The Frenchman looked into his eyes for a long moment, then turned back to Anne.

"And now I must go. At what time this evening?"

"Seven," she said. "We'll look forward to seeing you."

He went down the ladder into the speedboat and nodded to Jacaud. The engine roared into life and the boat turned away in a surge of power.

De Beaumont raised his hand in farewell, took a gold cigarette case from an inner pocket, selected a cigarette and lit it.

"Shall I tell Marcel to be ready to run you across tonight?" Jacaud said.

De Beaumont nodded. "And Pierre, but I shall also require you, Jacaud."

"Something interesting?"

"I have just seen a ghost," de Beaumont said calmly. "A ghost from the past, and ghosts are always interesting."

He settled back in the seat and Jacaud spun the wheel in his hands and took the speedboat round the point, his face quite expressionless.

Mallory stood at the wheel of *Foxhunter* thinking about de Beaumont. There had been something there, of that he was sure, but what could it possibly be? They had certainly never met.

The door clicked open behind him and Raoul Guyon came in and leaned against the chart table, lighting a cigarette.

"What did you think of him?"

Mallory shrugged. "Very charming, very elegant. Seems soft until you look in his eyes. Are you dining with them tonight?"

Guyon shook his head. "I've been invited for drinks afterwards. What was it like on the reef? Anything interesting?"

Mallory told him everything that had happened. When he had finished Guyon nodded. "From the sound of it, this cavern under the island would seem like an adequate hiding place for *L'Alouette*."

"That's what we'll have to find out."

"And how do we do that?"

"We'll use the aquamobiles. Try the Middle Passage approach I told you about."

"Straight into the cavern. Do you think they'll let us?"

"That's what we'll have to find out. We'll go in sometime tonight. The forecast's good and there's a moon. If the weather holds it shouldn't be too difficult. We'll go round the point in the dinghy. That should give us a good start."

Guyon sighed. "Legrande told me this one would be interesting. Little did he know. I'll see you later."

The door closed behind him and Mallory increased speed. The strange thing was that as *Foxhunter* ran back towards the jetty he wasn't thinking of the danger that lay ahead, of the long swim through the dark night. He was thinking of two metallic blue eyes and wondering what it was that he had seen in them.

8

●

The Man from Tangiers

THROUGH the french windows the lawn shimmered palely and the great beeches were silhouetted against the evening sky. Beyond was the timeless sad sough of the sea.

Inside, the room was warm and comfortable, the light softly diffused and a log hissed and spluttered on the hearthstone. There was a grand piano in one corner, two old comfortable couches drawn to the fire and a print or two on the walls.

It was a room that was lived in, a quiet, comfortable place, and the five people gathered loosely about the fire talked quietly to each other, Fiona Grant's occasional laugh breaking to the surface like a bubble of air in a quiet pool.

De Beaumont and his host wore dinner jackets and the Frenchman looked elegant, completely at his ease as he talked to Anne Grant and the General.

Fiona was wearing a simple green dress in some heavy silk material and sat on the arm of an old tapestry chair. Guyon stood beside her smoking a cigarette, one hand on the high mantelpiece. He was not in evening dress, but a well-cut suit of dark blue fitted his wiry figure to perfection, giving him a touch of distinction.

He leaned close to Fiona, muttered something in her ear, and she chuckled and stood up. "Raoul and I are going for a little walk. Anyone feel like joining us?"

"And what would you do if we said yes?" her father demanded.

"Brain you!" She kissed him affectionately and moved to the door. "I'll get a coat, Raoul. It could turn chilly."

Raoul smiled at de Beaumont. "Will I see you again before you leave, Colonel?"

De Beaumont shook his head. "Unlikely, I'm afraid. I keep early hours these days. Strict instructions from my doctor."

Guyon held out his hand. "For the present, then."

"And don't forget about that portrait," de Beaumont reminded him. "I meant what I said."

The young Frenchman nodded to the others and walked across to the door quickly as Fiona called from the hall.

"Seems a nice enough young chap," the General observed.

"Fiona obviously thinks so," Anne said. "And he's certainly talented. He was in the army in Algeria for several years before he took up painting."

"He's remarkably talented," de Beaumont said. "He'll make a name for himself with little difficulty."

The General turned his head as Jagbir came in and handed round drinks from a tray. "Any sign of Mr. Mallory yet?"

"No, General."

The General opened a silver box at his elbow and took out a long black cheroot. "I wonder what's happened to him?"

"Probably something to do with the boat," Anne said. "And he is walking, remember."

De Beaumont fitted a cigarette into a silver holder and said carefully, "Have you known him long?"

Hamish Grant shook his head. "Anne picked him up in Southampton. As a matter of fact, he got her out of a rather nasty scrape."

"And this is the basis upon which you hired him?"

"His papers were all in order. He'd only just signed off a tanker from Tampico a day or so before. Why do you ask?"

De Beaumont stood up, paced restlessly across to the french windows and turned. "This is really most difficult for me. I don't want you to think that I am interfering, yet on the other hand I feel that I should speak."

"You know something about him?" the General said. "Something to his discredit?"

De Beaumont came back to his chair and sat down. "You're aware, of course, that during the latter part of my army career I was commanding officer of a parachute regiment in Algeria. During the first few months of 1959 I was seconded to the general staff in Algiers and placed in charge of military security."

"How does this concern Mallory?"

"We kept a special file on people who were thought to be working for the F.L.N. or the various other nationalist organizations. Neil Mallory was in that file. He was captain of a sea-going motor-yacht berthed in Tangiers. He was a smuggler, engaged in the extremely profitable business of running contraband tobacco into Spain and Italy. He was also thought to be running guns for the F.L.N."

Hamish Grant emptied his glass, placed it carefully down on the table at his elbow and shrugged. "In other words he was a tough, rather unscrupulous young man who'd make a pound wherever there was one to be made. You've told me nothing I hadn't already worked out for myself." He pushed his glass across to Anne. "Pour me another, my dear."

"It was the years before Tangiers I found most interesting when I read this file," de Beaumont said. "That's why I recalled him so easily. Remember a book you loaned me about a year ago? A War Office manual entitled *A New Concept of Revolutionary Warfare*? You told me it had been written by a brilliant young officer in 1953 during the months following his release from a Chinese prison camp in Korea. I believe it caused quite a stir at the time."

The General stiffened, one hand tightening on the handle of his walking stick. "God in heaven," he said, "Mallory! Lieutenant-Colonel Neil Mallory."

"What was it they called him after that unpleasantness in Malaya?" de Beaumont said gently. "The Butcher of Perak?"

The glass into which Anne Grant was at that moment pouring whisky splintered sharply against the floor. She stood gazing fixedly at de Beaumont, a puzzled expression on her face, then crossed quickly to her father-in-law.

"What does he mean?"

Hamish Grant patted her hand. "You're sure it's the same man?"

De Beaumont shrugged. "The circumstances can hardly be coincidental. Admittedly, until today I had only seen his photograph, but it's a distinctive face. Not the sort one forgets easily."

"But what is it, Hamish?" Anne demanded.

De Beaumont was clearly embarrassed. "Perhaps it would be better if I went. Forgive me for having cast a shadow on what otherwise has been a truly delightful evening, but as a friend I felt that I had no choice but to tell you what I knew of this man."

"You were quite right." Hamish Grant got to his feet. "I'm very grateful to you. We'll see you again soon, I hope?"

"But of course."

The General sat down again and de Beaumont and Anne moved into the hall. "I'll get Jagbir to run you down to the jetty in the station wagon," she said.

De Beaumont shook his head. "No need. A fine evening. The walk will do me good."

When he raised her hand to his lips it was limp and unresponsive. He picked up his coat, opened the door and smiled. "Good night, Anne."

"Good night, Colonel de Beaumont," she said formally, and the door closed.

He stood on the top step, a slight smile on his face. She was annoyed because he had brought to light something discreditable in Mallory's past and that annoyance could only be the automatic reaction of a woman already deeply involved, which was interesting.

He moved down the steps towards the main gate and Jacaud stepped out of the bushes. "What happened?"

De Beaumont shrugged. "Patience, my dear Jacaud. I have set things in motion. Now we must await developments."

A foot crunched on gravel and Jacaud pulled him quickly into the shadows. A moment later Mallory walked by and went towards the house.

"What do we do now?" Jacaud whispered. "Return to St. Pierre?"

De Beaumont shook his head. "The night is young and interesting things have yet to happen. I think we will go down to the hotel and sample some of our good friend Owen's contraband brandy. We can await developments there."

He chuckled gently and led the way out through the gates to the narrow dirt road, white in the gloaming.

"Who was he, Hamish?" Anne said calmly. "I want to know."

"Neil Mallory?" Hamish shrugged. "An outstanding paratroop officer. First-rate war record, decorated several times. Afterwards, Palestine, Malaya, a different kind of war. He went to Korea in '51, was wounded and captured somewhere on the Imjin. Prisoner for two years."

"And then what?"

"From what one can make out he was the sort of man people were rather afraid of, especially his superiors. A little like Lawrence or Orde Wingate, God rest his soul. The sort of desperate eccentric who doesn't really fit in where peacetime soldiering's concerned."

"De Beaumont said he was a colonel? He must have been very young."

"Probably the youngest in the army at the time. He wrote this book *A New Concept of Revolutionary Warfare* for the War Office in 1953. It aroused a lot of talk at the time. Most people seemed to think he'd turned Communist. Kept quoting from Mao Tse-tung's book on guerrilla warfare as if the damned thing were a bible."

"What happened?"

"He'd been promoted lieutenant-colonel after the Korean business. They had to find him something to do so they sent him to Malaya. Things weren't too good at that time. In some areas the Communist guerrillas virtually controlled everything. They gave Mallory command of some local troops. It wasn't really a regiment. Not much more than a hundred men. Recruiting was bad at the time. Little stocky Malayan peasants straight out of the rice fields. I know the type."

"Did they make good soldiers?"

"In three months they were probably the most formidable jungle troops in Malaya. Within six they'd proved themselves so efficient in the field they'd earned a nickname: 'Mallory's Tigers'."

"What happened in Perak?"

"The climax of the drama, or the tragedy, if you like, because that's what it was. At that time Perak was rotten with Communist guerrillas, especially on the border with Thailand. The powers-that-be told Mallory to go in and clean them out once and for all."

"And did he?"

"I think you could say that, but when he'd finished he'd earned himself a new name."

"The Butcher of Perak?"

"That's right. A man who'd ordered the shooting of many prisoners, who had interrogated and tortured captives in custody. A man who was proved to have acted with a singleminded and quite cold-blooded ferocity."

"And he was cashiered?"

The General shook his head. "I should imagine that would have involved others. No, they simply retired him. Gave the usual sort of story to the newspapers. Took the line that he'd never really recovered from his experiences in Chinese hands and so on. Nobody could argue with that and the whole thing simply faded away."

She sat staring into the fire for several moments, then

shook her head. "The man you describe must have been
a monster, and Neil Mallory isn't that, I'm sure."

He stretched out a hand and covered hers. "You're
attracted to him, aren't you?" She made no reply and he
sighed. "God knows it was bound to happen. A long time
since Angus went, Anne. A long, long time."

The door opened and Jagbir appeared, Mallory at
his shoulder. "Mr. Mallory is here, General."

Hamish Grant straightened in his chair, shoulders
squared, and said calmly, "Show Colonel Mallory in, Jagbir."

Mallory paused just inside the room, his face very
white in the soft light, the strange dark eyes showing
nothing. "Who told you?"

"De Beaumont," the General said. "When he was head
of French Military Intelligence in Algiers in '59 they had
a general file on people like you. I understand you were
running guns out of Tangiers to the F.L.N. Is that correct?"

For the moment Mallory was aware only of a feeling of
profound relief. That de Beaumont should recognize him
from the North African days was unfortunate, but at least
the front he had used in Tangiers had obviously been
accepted and that was the main thing.

"Does it matter?" he said. "My past, I mean?"

"Good heavens, man, I'm not interested in what you
got up to in Tangiers. It's what happened in Perak that I
want to know about."

"And suppose I say that's none of your damned business?"

The old man stayed surprisingly calm, but Anne moved
forward and touched Mallory on the sleeve. "Please, Neil,
I must know."

Her eyes seemed very large as she gazed up at him, and
he turned abruptly, crossed to the french window and went
down the steps of the terrace outside.

He stood at the wall above the inlet in the desolate
light of gloaming, and, below, the lights of a ship out to
sea seemed very far away.

He was tired, drained of all emotion, aware out of

some strange inner knowledge that whatever a man did came to nothing in the final analysis.

A step sounded on gravel behind him. When he turned, Hamish Grant and his daughter-in-law were standing at the bottom of the steps. They moved to the table, the old man lowered himself into one of the chairs and Anne Grant approached Mallory.

For a long time she stood peering up at him, her face in shadow, and then she swayed forward, burying her face against his chest, and his arms went round her instinctively.

The old man was silhouetted sharply against the pale night sky and the sea, hands crossed on top of his stick, rooted into the ground like some ancient statue.

"Right, Colonel Mallory," he said in a voice that would brook no denial, "I'm ready when you are."

9

●

The Butcher of Perak

LIEUTENANT Gregson paced nervously up and down, smoking a cigarette, trying to look as unconcerned as the half-dozen Malay soldiers who squatted in the long grass talking quietly. At the edge of the clearing the body of a man was suspended by his ankles above the smouldering embers of a fire, the flesh peeling from his skull.

The smell was nauseating, so bad that Gregson could almost taste it. He shuddered visibly and wondered what was keeping the Colonel. He was only twenty-two, slim with good shoulders but the face beneath the red beret was fine-drawn, the eyes set too deeply in their sockets.

He heard the sound of the Land Rover coming along the track and snapped his fingers quickly. There was no need. The soldiers had risen as one man with the easy, relaxed discipline of veterans and stood waiting. A moment later Sergeant Tewak pushed his way into the clearing, followed by the Colonel.

Mallory wore a paratrooper's beret and a camouflaged uniform open at the neck, no badges of rank in evidence. He stood staring at the body, dark eyes brooding in that strange white face, and restlessly tapped a bamboo swagger stick against his right knee.

When he spoke his voice was calm. "When did you find him?"

"About an hour ago. I thought you might want to see him exactly as they left him."

Mallory nodded. "Leave Sergeant Tewak in charge here. He can bring the body into Maluban in your Land Rover. You can come back with me."

He turned abruptly into the jungle and Gregson gave the necessary orders to Tewak and followed. When he reached the Land Rover Mallory was already sitting behind the wheel and Gregson climbed into the passenger seat.

The Colonel drove away rapidly and Gregson lit a cigarette and said carefully, "I hope you're not blaming yourself in any way, sir?"

Mallory shook his head. "He was a good soldier, he knew the risks he was taking. If they'd accepted him we'd have learned a hell of a lot. Probably enough to have put them out of business in the whole of Perak. But they didn't."

Remembering the pathetic, tortured body, the stench of burning flesh, Gregson shuddered. "They didn't give him much of a chance, did they, sir?"

"They seldom do," Mallory observed dryly. "There are one or two chairborne flunkeys in Singapore who could have learned something this afternoon. Unfortunately they never seem to come this far in." He took a cigarette from his breast pocket, one hand on the wheel, and lit it. "There was a signal from H.Q. while you were away. They're sending me a plane Friday. There's to be an enquiry."

Gregson turned quickly. "The Kelantang affair?"

Mallory nodded. "Apparently the papers got hold of it back home." He slowed to negotiate a steep hill. "I don't think I'll be coming back."

"But that's ridiculous," Gregson said angrily. "There isn't a guerrilla left in Kelantang. The Tigers have had more success in six months than any other unit since the emergency began."

"They don't like my methods," Mallory said. "It's as simple as that."

"Neither did I, at first, but I know now that it's the only way. If you don't fight fire with fire you might as well pack up and go home."

"And they won't let us do either," Mallory said. "Britain never likes to let go of anything. That's my Irish father speaking and he had the best of reasons for knowing."

The Land Rover went over a small rise as it emerged from the jungle, and beneath them, beside the river, was Maluban. There were perhaps forty or fifty thatched houses on stilts, the saw-mill and rubber warehouse on the far side of the jetty.

It was very still, the jungle brooding in that quiet period before night fell, and as Mallory took the Land Rover down into the village a whistle sounded shrilly and the workers started to emerge from the mill.

He braked to a halt outside his command post, a weathered, clapboard bungalow raised on concrete stilts, saluted the sentry and ran up the steps briskly. Inside, a corporal sat at a radio transmitter in one corner. He started to rise and Mallory pushed him down.

"Anything?" he asked in Malayan.

"Not since you left, sir."

Mallory moved to the large map of the area which was pinned to one wall. He ran a finger along the course of the river. "Jack must be about there now. A good forty miles."

Gregson nodded and indicated a small village to the southwest. "Harry should be at Trebu by nightfall. Between them they'll have swept most of the western side of the river."

"Without turning up a damned thing. What's our effective strength here at the moment?"

"Including Sergeant Tewak and the six men bringing in the body, a dozen. Eight men in the sick-bay and all genuine."

"You don't need to tell me." Mallory picked up his

swagger stick. "Mr. Li's giving a dinner party tonight. I'll probably be there till midnight. Call me if anything turns up."

"Something special?"

Mallory nodded. "He's got a journalist staying with him for a few days. A woman called Mary Hume."

"Isn't she the one who used to be an M.P.?"

"That's right. One of these professional liberals who spend their time visiting the trouble spots and kicking the poor old army up the backside in print."

"Never mind," Gregson said. "Old Li's food is always interesting."

"Some consolation." Mallory moved to the door, turned and, for almost the first time since Gregson had known him, smiled. "Friday—that's just three days. Not much time to clean up Perak, eh?"

When he had gone Gregson went back to the map. There was a hell of a lot of country and he knew in his bones that the patrols they had out along the river were wasting their time. There were perhaps sixty Chinese guerrillas in Perak, certainly no more. And yet they were enough to terrorize an entire state, to fill the people themselves with such fear that all hopes of co-operation were impossible.

And on Friday the Colonel was to fly to Kuala Lumpur to face an enquiry that could well lead to his court-martial and disgrace. Gregson cursed softly. If only Mallory could have flown out with the news that he and his Tigers had done it again. Had destroyed the last effective guerrilla band in the north. That would have given them something to think about at H.Q.

He went into the bedroom at the rear, poured himself a drink and stood on the verandah looking across the small strip of rough grass that was the garden. A loose board creaked and he turned and saw Suwon, Mr. Li's secretary, coming up the steps.

She was perhaps twenty and her skin had that creamy look peculiar to Eurasian women, her lips an extra fullness that gave her a faintly sensual air. Her scarlet dress was of heavy red silk, slashed on either side above the knee, and moulded her ripe figure.

He grinned crookedly and raised his glass. "Surprise, surprise. I thought you'd be at the party."

"I will be later," she said. "But I wanted to see you."

"Now that's most flattering."

He moved close and she held a hand against his chest. "Please, Jack, this is serious. The wife of Sabal, the ferryman, has just been to see me. She's scared out of her wits."

"What's the trouble?"

"They've been hiding a wounded terrorist at their house for three days now, under the usual threats. He was shot in that patrol clash on the other side of the river last week. His friends took him to Sabal's house because of its isolation. You know where it is?"

Gregson's stomach was hollow with excitement and when he put down his glass his hand was shaking. "About half a mile upriver. So they've decided to hand him over?"

She shrugged. "If the man doesn't have medical treatment soon he'll die. Sabal is a Buddhist. He couldn't let that happen."

"You've told no one else?"

She shook her head. "I've no desire to become a target. You know how easily these things leak out. That's why I came the back way."

He buckled on his belt and revolver. "No one will know who tipped me off, I promise you that."

"It's Sabal and his family I'm really worried about."

"No need to be. I'll only take a couple of men with me. Make it look like a routine call." He kissed her lightly on the mouth. "You'd better get going. They'll be looking for you at dinner. And not a word about this to anyone. I'd like to surprise the Colonel."

He went out through the other room and she heard his voice raised as he called to the duty corporal. A few moments later the Land Rover drove away. She stood there, a shadow slanting across her eyes like a mask. It was as if she were waiting for something. Only when the sound of the engine had finally died into the distance did she turn and walk away.

A moth fluttered despairingly beside the oil lamp and shrivelled in the heat. What was left of it fluttered to the table. Mr. Li brushed it away and reached for the decanter. It was obvious that he had European blood in him. His eyes lifted slightly at the corners, but they were shrewd and kindly, the lips beneath the straight nose well formed and full of humour.

"More brandy, Mrs. Hume?"

She was in her early forties, her greying hair cut short in the current fashion, still attractive in her simple print dress, a kashmir shawl around her shoulders against the cool of the evening.

She pushed her glass across and Mr. Li continued, "You have no idea of the pleasure it gives me to entertain a British Member of Parliament in my own home."

"I'm afraid you're a little out of date, Mr. Li," she answered lightly as Suwon came in with the coffee. "I'm no longer interested in politics. Simply a working journalist on an assignment."

"To discover for yourself the state of things in the border country?" Mr. Li smiled. "How fortunate that Colonel Mallory agreed to accept my hospitality during his stay. I am sure there can be no greater authority on the troubled times through which we are passing."

"I've already seen something of Colonel Mallory's methods," Mary Hume said coldly, and turned to Mallory, who sat at one end of the long table in a beautifully tailored drill uniform, the medal ribbons and S.A.S. wings above his left pocket a splash of colour in the lamplight. "I drove through a village called Pedak about ten miles south of here on the way in. Every house burned to the ground on your orders. Women and children homeless and the rains due."

Suwon leaned over Mallory's shoulder to pour coffee into his cup and he was aware of her fragrance. "One of my patrols was ambushed in Pedak two days ago. Four men killed and two wounded. The villagers could have warned them. They didn't."

"Because they were afraid," she said angrily. "Surely that's obvious. The Communist guerrillas must have forced them to keep silent with threats."

"Quite right," Mallory replied calmly. "That's why I burned their houses. Next time they'll think twice."

"But you're giving them an impossible choice," she said. "To betray their own countrymen."

"Something people like you never seem to get straight. The men who were ambushed and killed, my soldiers, were Malays. The guerrillas who killed them are Chinese."

"Not all of them."

"Some are Malayan Chinese, I wouldn't argue on that point, but the majority are Chinese Communists, trained and armed by the Army of the People's Republic and infiltrated into Malaya from Thailand."

"What Colonel Mallory says is quite true, Mrs. Hume," Mr. Li put in. "These terrorists are bad people. They have made things very difficult for us in this area."

"For business, you mean," she said acidly.

"But of course." Mr. Li was not at all put out. "Many of the great rubber estates have virtually gone out of business and things will soon be as bad in the timber trade. At the mill my workers are already on half-time. These are the people who really suffer, you know. Two weeks ago the Catholic mission at Kota Banu was attacked. The priest-in-charge was away at the time, but two nuns and thirteen young girls were killed."

"You're wasting your time, Li," Mallory said. "That isn't the sort of story Mrs. Hume wants to hear. That rag of hers usually prints items like that in the bottom left-hand corner of page seven."

He picked up his brandy and walked out on the open verandah, aware of Li's voice raised in apology behind him. In the gathering darkness beyond the river the jungle started to come alive, tree-frogs setting the air vibrating, while howler monkeys challenged each other, swinging through the trees, and through it all the steady, pulsating beat of the crickets.

At his shoulder Mary Hume said in a dry, matter-of-fact voice: "They're saying in Singapore that you executed your prisoners during the Kelantang operation. Is it true?"

"I was hard on the heels of another gang. I needed every man I had." Mallory shrugged. "Prisoners would have delayed me."

"And now there's to be an enquiry. They'll kick you out, you know."

He shrugged. "Isn't that what you want?"

She frowned. "You don't like me, do you, Colonel Mallory?"

"Not particularly."

"May I ask why? I'm only doing my job."

"As I remember, that was the excuse you offered in Korea when you and one or two choice specimens like you accepted an invitation from the Chinese to see what things were really like over on that side."

"I see now," she said, and her voice died away in a long sigh.

"You wrote some excellent articles on how good the prison camps were," Mallory said. "How well we were all treated. I read them after I was released. Of course, they never showed you over my camp, Mrs. Hume, which is hardly surprising. Around about the time you were starting your conducted tour I was doing six months in a rather small bamboo cage. As a matter of fact, about twenty of us were. A salutary experience, particularly as winter was just beginning."

"I reported the facts as I saw them," she said calmly.

"People like you always do." He swallowed about half of his brandy and went on: "One thing really does interest me. Why has it always got to be your own country? Why is it never the other side? I mean, what exactly *is* eating away at your guts?"

She was obviously only controlling her anger by a supreme effort of will, and when she replied her voice vibrated slightly. "Where a moral principle is involved I refuse to be hampered by a spurious nationalism."

"Is that a fact?" Mallory said. "Well, I've got news for

you, Mrs. Hume. I'd rather have that lot out there in the jungle than you and your kind any day. At least they fight for what they believe in. I can respect them for that."

"Even when they butcher nuns and young girls?" she taunted.

"We managed things like that on a much more impressive scale during the war. After all, for a purist like yourself there can't be much difference between the terrorist's grenade and the bombs released at the touch of a button from forty thousand feet." She was suddenly very still and he said softly: "But then I was forgetting. Wasn't your husband a bomber pilot during the war? I'm sure his opinion would be most interesting."

"My husband is dead, Colonel Mallory. He was killed in the war."

"I know, Mrs. Hume," Mallory said softly.

She turned abruptly and went back inside and Mallory took out a cigarette, striking a match against the verandah rail.

There was a rustle in the bushes below and Sergeant Tewak said quietly: "Colonel, there is bad news at the command post. It would be well for you to come."

Mallory glanced over his shoulder quickly. Mr. Li and Mary Hume sat at the table, talking earnestly, heads together, and Suwon busied herself preparing drinks at the sideboard. He vaulted over the rail and followed Tewak through the bushes.

The little Malay hurried along without speaking, leading the way out through the rear gate and down the hill to the village. The streets were quiet, but outside the command post Mallory found what seemed to be the whole detachment standing in twos and threes, each man armed and in marching order.

As Tewak led the way round to the store hut at the side of the bungalow Mallory was aware of the emptiness that snatched at the pit of his stomach. The Malay opened the door, switched on the light and led the way in.

The body was covered by a groundsheet and lay on a trestle table in the centre of the room. Mallory knew it was Gregson at once because of the American paratrooper's boots which he had bought at a second-hand shop in Singapore three months previously. Tewak pulled back the groundsheet and waited, his face like stone.

The teeth were clenched, lips drawn back in the death-agony. His hands had been tied behind him, the eyes gouged out, quite obviously while he was still alive. The rest of him was like a piece of raw meat.

Mallory took a deep breath and turned away. "When did it happen?"

"About half an hour ago. He was tipped off that a wounded terrorist was hiding at the house of Sabal the ferryman. I arrived back about an hour after he'd left. He only took two men. When he didn't return I thought I'd better investigate."

"Are they all dead?"

"Also Sabal and his wife and their four children."

Mallory nodded slowly, a slight frown on his face. He looked down at the body on the table, once more covered with the groundsheet.

"Go to Mr. Li's bungalow. There's an Englishwoman there, a Mrs. Hume. Tell her I want to see her. If she refuses to come use force."

The door closed softly and Mallory took out a cigarette and lit it, thinking about Gregson, about the senseless, needless cruelty of his going. It had been intended as a threat, so much was obvious, and had been directed at him personally. Whoever controlled the sixty or so terrorists in Perak had simply used Gregson as a calling card.

A few minutes later the door opened and Mary Hume was pushed inside. Behind her Mallory was conscious of Li's troubled face in the doorway.

She was trembling with anger, her face very white as she moved forward. Mallory cut in quickly before she could speak.

"So sorry to trouble you, Mrs. Hume, but one of my young officers was very anxious to meet you."

As the frown deepened across her forehead, he pulled the groundsheet away quickly. She stood staring at the table, an expression of wonderment frozen into place, and then her head started to move from side to side, the lips trembling. Mr. Li took her gently in his arms and held her close.

"This was not a good thing to do, Colonel."

"You go to hell," Mallory said, "and you can take her with you," and he turned and covered Gregson carefully.

In the distance thunder rumbled and then lightning flared. In the split second of its illumination Mallory saw each item of furniture in his bedroom clearly. He tossed his swagger stick and beret on the bed and opened the shutters. As he stepped on to the verandah the rain came with a sudden, great rush, filling the air with its voice.

He breathed deeply, taking the air into his lungs, and a quiet voice said, "The night air is not good when the rains start, Colonel."

Suwon stood a few feet away by the rail and as lightning flared again her face seemed to jump out of the darkness, the embroidered dragon on the scarlet dress coming alive like some strange night creature.

"I was hoping you'd come," he said.

She moved very close until their bodies touched and her scent was warm in his nostrils, the sharply pointed breasts hard against him. She placed one hand behind his neck, her mouth slack with desire, and he said softly, "Why did you tell Gregson that a wounded terrorist was hiding out at Sabal's house?"

As his hands slid round to the small of her back her body tensed, taut as a bow-string. She gave a terrified gasp, turned and stumbled down the steps to the lawn. As she started across, lightning exploded again and in that brief moment of illumination Sergeant Tewak and half a dozen men moved forward in a semicircle. As Tewak reeched her the sky seemed to split wide open with a crash of thunder that made the earth tremble, drowning her cry of terror as she was turned roughly and pushed towards the steps.

In his room Mallory lit the lamp, pulled out a chair and sat down. Suwon's dress was saturated, clinging to her like a second skin, and her face was very white as Tewak brought her forward.

"Earlier this evening you visited the command post by

way of the garden. You told Lieutenant Gregson there was a wounded terrorist at Sabal's house." She started to shake her head weakly in denial and Mallory went on: "Don't waste time in stupid lies. The duty corporal overheard the entire conversation."

Tears started to roll down her face and he said: "Gregson is dead, but I don't blame you for that. Only the person who gave you your orders. Who was it? You needn't be afraid. I'll see you're protected."

She shook her head desperately and tried to pull free from Tewak's iron grip. She was wasting her time. The Malay raised his eyebrows. Mallory nodded and Tewak smashed his clenched fist into her mouth, sending her staggering across the room on to the bed.

When Mallory pulled her forward her lips were crushed and bleeding and a couple of teeth were missing.

"Two weeks ago your friends burned down a Catholic mission and butchered thirteen little girls," he said calmly. "Last July they derailed a train and killed or injured nearly a hundred peasants. As far as I'm concerned you're expendable. Now either you tell me what I want to know or I'll let Tewak really go to work on you, and one thing I can promise—you'll never want to look in a mirror again."

Tewak started to take off his belt and she shook her head weakly, the breath bubbling out through her broken mouth.

"Mr. Li," she moaned. "It was Mr. Li."

Li examined himself in the bathroom mirror, a pair of tweezers in one hand. Very carefully he plucked a couple of gold hairs from his upper lip, then opened a large, gold-capped bottle of perfumed astringent and poured some into his palms. He carefully massaged his face, wincing slightly at the stinging coldness, turned and moved into his bedroom.

Mallory was standing by the open window that led to the verandah. He wore his red beret and the swagger stick in his right hand beat restlessly against his thigh. It was the eyes which told Li his fate, those strange, unfathomable eyes like holes in the white face, staring through and beyond him.

There was nothing to say, nothing at all. He stood there, a slight, careful smile on his face, hands thrust into the pockets of his silk dressing-gown, and Mallory made a slight gesture with his hand that brought Tewak and his men into the room.

Mr. Li moved to a small coffee table, selected a cigarette from a jade box and lit it. "Who told you?"

Mallory shook his head. "Suwon was a mistake. Girls like her value their looks too much. They haven't got anything else to trade with."

The bookcase against the far wall came down with a splintering crash and three of the soldiers rammed the butt ends of their rifles against the wooden panelling. A moment later a large segment fell out, revealing a cupboard, perhaps three feet square, containing a wireless transmitter and several files.

Mallory examined the find, nodded and turned quickly. "So far, so good. Now let's get down to business. According to our intelligence reports you have between sixty and seventy guerrillas operating in Perak. I'd like to know where they are."

"You're wasting your time, my dear Mallory," Li said. "And that's something you can't really spare, isn't it? When is it they're coming for you—Friday? Thirty-six hours, that's all."

He started to laugh and Tewak raised a hand. Mallory shook his head. "No sense in wasting time on the preliminaries. Bring him into the living-room, there's a fire there."

Li was aware of a coldness clutching at his inside. The stories he had heard about this man Mallory, of his Tigers and the way they operated. No one really believed it because the English didn't fight in this way. Didn't use such methods, which was their greatest weakness. Brainwashing and psychological pressures he had been prepared for, but this . . . !

They hustled him into the other room and across to the wide stone fireplace in which he had ordered the servants to light a log fire against the dampness of the rains. Mallory nodded and Li's dressing-gown and pyjama jacket were ripped away, baring him to the waist. His hands were jerked roughly behind his back and lashed with a length of rope.

There was a disturbance outside the door and Mallory heard Mary Hume's voice raised shrilly. He crossed the room and moved past his men into the corridor. The dark circles under her eyes accentuated the paleness of her face and she had obviously been crying.

"What's going on in there?" she said. "I demand to know."

"I'm questioning Mr. Li," Mallory told her. "We've just discovered that he's not quite what he seems to be."

"I don't believe you," she said.

"Well, that's just too bad. At a later date I'll be happy to show you the transmitting set he had hidden in his room, but right now I'm busy." He turned to the corporal on his left. "Escort Mrs. Hume to her room and see that she doesn't leave it."

He went back into the living-room, slamming the door on her sudden, indignant outburst, and crossed to the fire. He sat down in the chair opposite Li, took out a cigarette and lit it.

"Have you ever been tortured?" Li made no reply and Mallory continued: "In 1943 I was working under cover in France. I was only twenty. The Gestapo got hold of me. The first two days I didn't do too bad, but by the end of the week I was telling them everything they wanted to know. Of course, by that time London had changed everything round, so it didn't really matter."

"How very interesting," Li said.

"I thought you might say that." Mallory picked up a poker and inserted it into the fire. "I'm afraid I can't wait for a week, you understand that, but I don't think I'll have to. I've had the extra advantage of two years in a Communist prison camp. They taught me a lot, those friends of yours."

Li gazed at the poker in fascinated horror and his throat went dry. He moistened his lips and croaked: "You wouldn't dare. The marks would be on my body for all to see. Mrs. Hume would be a witness to all that had taken place."

"They told me to clean out Perak," Mallory said, "and I've only got till Friday morning to do it. That means cutting a few corners. You understand, I'm sure."

He took the poker from the fire. It was white hot and he turned and said gently, "Tell me where your men are, that's all I want to know."

"You're wasting your time," Li said. "You might as well shoot me and get it over with."

"I don't think so." Mallory considered him carefully and shook his head. "I'd say you might last two hours, but I doubt it."

It was perhaps three hours later when Li regained consciousness on his bed in the cool darkness of his room. His hands had been roughly bandaged and pain coursed through his entire body, sending his senses reeling.

And he had talked. That was the shameful thing. He had poured out everything to the terrible Englishman with the white face and the dark eyes that pierced straight through to the soul.

He pushed himself upright and slowly hobbled across the floor, grinding his teeth together to keep from crying out. He paused at the window and peered outside. The verandah was deserted. There was no one in sight. He pushed the window open and crossed to the steps. He stood there for a moment, inhaling the freshness of the rain, a faint excitement stirring inside him, driving the pain from his mind. He would win. He would beat Mallory in the end and that was the important thing.

He stumbled down the steps and started across the lawn. He was perhaps half-way across when he heard the click of a bolt as a weapon was cocked. He turned, mouth opening to cry out, conscious that even now Mallory had won.

The line of fire erupting from the bushes spun him around twice and drove him down against the earth. For a moment only there was the scent of wet grass in his nostrils, then nothing.

In his office at the command post Mallory heard the rattle of the sub-machine-gun clearly. He paused for a moment, head raised, then returned to the map in front of him. A few minutes later the door opened and Tewak entered, shaking rain from his groundsheet.

Mallory sat back. "What happened?"

"The sentry got him as he was crossing the garden. Mrs. Hume's outside. Apparently she ran out of the house when she heard the shooting. She saw his condition."

"Bring her in," Mallory said.

She was wearing an old Burberry that was far too big for her, the shoulders soaked by the rain. Tewak led her forward and she slumped into a chair and sat looking at Mallory, her face old and careworn.

"I saw Mr. Li," she said dully. "I saw what you'd done to him."

"Mr. Li was directly responsible for the murder by torture of Lieutenant Gregson and his men," Mallory said. "He was responsible for the deaths of thirteen schoolgirls two weeks ago and very many more innocent people during the past two years."

"You tortured him," she said. "Tortured him in cold blood, then shot him down."

"If he'd gone to Singapore he'd have been tried and very probably sentenced to ten years at the most as a political offender," Mallory said. "His friends would have got him out before then, believe me."

"You fool," she whispered. "You've lost everything. Everything. Don't you see that?"

Mallory leaned forward. "There are sixty-three Communist guerrillas in Perak, Mrs. Hume. That's something I got out of Li. About thirty of them are camped at this moment on an abandoned rubber estate near Trebu. I've got a large patrol in that area now. They'll be in position to attack at 2 a.m. The rest are going to pass downriver hidden in two fishing boats within the next hour. Apparently, they'd intended to destroy the railway bridge at Pegu at dawn. I'm afraid they'll be disappointed."

She frowned slightly, as if finding difficulty in taking in what he had said. "But you've only got a handful of men.

You can't possibly hope to defeat such a large group."

"Solicitude for my welfare at this stage, Mrs. Hume? You're slipping." He got to his feet and buckled on his revolver. "Don't worry, we have our ways." He crossed to the door, opened it and turned. "Stay here, and this time I mean it."

Mary Hume opened her mouth to protest, but no sound came, and suddenly she was afraid. Afraid of this terrible young man. There was nothing she could do, nothing to prevent the tragedy that was taking place. Out of some strange, inner knowledge she knew that Neil Mallory, in the process of destroying the evil that he hated, was also destroying himself. The most surprising thing of all was that she cared.

Mallory moved across to the jetty and paused beside the two men who squatted behind the heavy machine-gun. Another was positioned on top of a small hill fifty yards away and between them they covered the river with an arc of fire.

At the end of the jetty Tewak waited with the rest of the men. Two of them crouched behind the narrow wall, the heavy tanks of their flame-throwers bulging obscenely.

The rain rushed into the river with a heavy, sibilant whispering, and Mallory was aware of a strange, aching sadness. It was as if he had done all this before in another time, another place. As if life were a circle turning endlessly. Everything that had happened during the previous few hours lacked definition, like a dream only half remembered.

And then Tewak grunted. There was the slapping of water against a keel, a sensation of an even darker mass moving through the darkness, and Mallory tapped Tewak lightly on the shoulder.

The little sergeant picked up a portable spot and switched it on. The white beam lanced through the night, picking out two large fishing boats as they slipped downstream, side by side, sails furled, a man in each stern working a sweep.

There was a cry of alarm and the first boat half lifted out of the water as it collided with the ferry hawser which

Tewak and his men had suspended across the river an hour earlier.

The boat spun round, crashing into its fellow, and there was another cry, followed by a burst of small-arms fire directed towards the jetty.

Mallory called out and the men with the flame-throwers stood up. Liquid fire arched through the night, splashing across the two boats. Immediately their super-structure and sails started to burn and men poured on to their decks from below.

The two heavy machine-guns opened up, raking the decks, chopping down the guerrillas as soon as they appeared. Tewak dropped the spot, picked up his sub-machine-gun and joined in with the rest of the men.

It was over within a few minutes. A handful jumped from the blazing inferno and struck out desperately for safety, but the flame-throwers searched them out, the fire licking hungrily across the surface of the water, catching them one by one.

By this time the river and the village were brilliantly illuminated and Mallory stood there watching, taking no part in what was happening. He glanced at his watch. It was just after 2 a.m. and he wondered how Harrison was getting on.

He turned and found Mary Hume standing a few yards away. When he walked towards her he saw that she was crying.

"You butcher," she said. "You butcher. I'll see you hang for this night's work."

"I'm sure you will, Mrs. Hume," he said calmly and went past her along the jetty.

Twenty-four hours left now till that plane arrived, that was all, but it was enough. If he moved fast along the river bank to meet up with Harrison and his men coming south they'd be certain to sweep up any survivors of the clash at the rubber estate. Another twenty-four hours and after that . . .

As he went up the bank towards the command post the first fishing boat sank beneath the surface with a hiss of steam.

10

•

An Affair of Honour

A MATCH flared outlining Hamish Grant's craggy features as he lit a cheroot. "And the enquiry?"

It was quite dark now, and, below, waves creamed over the rocks in the entrance of the tiny inlet. It was a warm, soft night, stars strung away to the horizon, and when a cloud moved from the face of the moon the terrace was bathed in a hard, white light.

Mallory turned from looking out to sea and shrugged. "A foregone conclusion. They used terms like: 'Previous gallant service.' Hinted that I hadn't really recovered from the ordeal of two years in a Chinese prison camp."

"And spared you the ultimate disgrace."

"They didn't actually cashier me, if that's what you mean. You could say I was eased into retirement as quietly as possible. For the good of the service, of course."

"Naturally," the old man said. "A bad business. That sort of thing rubs off on everyone concerned."

"What I did to Li he would have done to me," Mallory said. "The purpose of terrorism is to terrorize. Lenin said that. It's on page one of every Communist handbook on revolutionary warfare. You can only fight that kind of fire with fire. Otherwise you might as well lie down and let the waves wash over you. That's what I brought out of that Chinese prison camp, General."

"An interesting point of view."

"The only one in the circumstances. I did what had to be done. When I'd finished there was no more terror by night in Perak. No more Kota Banus. No more butchering of little girls. God knows, that should count for something."

There was silence. In the moonlight Anne Grant's face seemed very pale, the eyes dark and secret, telling him nothing. When a cloud crossed the moon she became a motionless silhouette, her face turned towards him, but still she didn't speak.

Mallory sighed and tossed his cigarette over the wall in a glowing curve. "Under the circumstances, perhaps you'll excuse me, General? This has turned out to be one of those evenings when I could do with a drink."

He turned and went up the steps, the sound of his going fading quickly into the darkness. After a while Hamish Grant said quietly: "It's not often one meets a man like that. Someone who's willing to carry the guilt for the rest of us. It takes a rather special brand of courage."

She turned towards him, her face a pale blur, and then, as if coming to a decision, stood up. "Do you mind?"

He reached for her hand and held it tightly. "Leave me the car, will you? I might join you later."

And that was that, Mallory told himself. *That was very much that.* No question of what she had thought of him. Her silence, that stillness, had been answer enough. And the strange thing was that it mattered, that for the first time in years the protective shell he had grown had cracked and now he was defenceless.

His chin was on his breast, hands in pockets, as he turned on to the springy turf beside the road, white in the moonlight that ran down to the harbour.

A small wind seemed to crawl across his face and he drew in his breath sharply. He heard no sound and yet he knew that she walked beside him. He spoke calmly, but with a faint Irish intonation, inherited from his father, always apparent in moments of great stress.

"And what would you be wanting, Anne Grant?"

"A drink, Neil Mallory," she said, matching his mood, "and perhaps another. Would that be asking too much?"

He paused and turned to face her, hands still thrust into his pockets. In the moonlight she looked very beautiful, more beautiful than he had ever thought a woman could be, and there were tears in her eyes. He slipped an arm about her shoulders and together they went down the hill towards the lights of the hotel.

In the long grass on the hill above the cliffs Raoul Guyon lay on his back and stared into an infinity of stars, his hands clasped behind his head. Beside him Fiona Grant sat cross-legged, combing her hair.

She turned and smiled, her face clear in the moonlight. "Well, are you going to make an honest woman of me?"

"As always, you have a gift for the difficult question," he said.

"A plain yes or no would do. I'm reasonably civilized."

"A word no woman is entitled to use," he said solemnly, and lit a cigarette. "Life is seldom as simple as yes or no, Fiona."

"I don't agree," she said. "It's people who make it complicated. My father likes you, if that's got anything to do with it, and I can't see what they'd have to complain about at your end. After all, I could pass for French."

"I'm quite sure my mother would adore you. On the other hand, we Bretons are very old-fashioned in certain matters. She would never allow me to marry a girl who couldn't bring a sizable dowry with her."

"Would eleven thousand pounds do?" Fiona said. "My favourite uncle died last March."

"I'm sure *Maman* would be most impressed," Guyon told her.

She squirmed against him, laying her head on his chest. "In any case, why should we worry about money? I know most artists have to struggle, but how many of them paint like you?"

"A good point."

And she was right. Already he had sold many paintings, working between assignments on the family farm near Loudeac that his mother still managed so competently. Mornings on the banks of the Oust with leaves drifting from the beech trees into the river and the smell of wet earth. Country that he had grown up in and loved. He was aware, with a strange wonderment, that he wanted to take this girl there, to see again with her the old grey farmhouse rooted into its hollow amongst the trees, walk with her over the familiar country that he loved so much.

"Of course, there could always be someone else," she said.

Her voice was light and yet there was a poignancy there. It was as if she was aware of how near to hurt she might be, and he pulled her close instinctively.

"There was a girl once, Fiona, in Algiers a long time ago. She gave me peace when I needed it more than anything else on earth. She paid for that gift with her life. A high price. I've been trying to escape from her ever since."

There was a short silence, and then she said gently: "Have you ever considered that it might be Algeria that you're running from? That somehow this girl has come to symbolize everything that ever happened there?"

In that single instant he knew that what she had said was true. That by some strange perception she had struck right to the very heart of things.

"I know I'm young, Raoul," she continued, "and on the whole I've only seen the lighter side, but I know this: the war in Algeria wasn't the first to send men home with blood on their hands and it won't be the last. But that's life. There wouldn't be any sweet without sour. People get by."

"At a guess I'd say you must be about a thousand years old."

He kissed her passionately and she linked her arms behind his neck and pressed her body against him. After a while she rolled away and lay on her back, breathless, eyes sparkling.

"And now do you think I might get to see that farm in Brittany?"

He pulled her to her feet and held her at arm's length. "Did I ever have a choice?"

She reached up to kiss him and then turned and ran away down the hill. Guyon gave her a start of perhaps twenty yards and then went after her, laughter bubbling up spontaneously inside him for the first time in years.

The bar at the hotel was a long, pleasant room with whitewashed walls, its windows facing out to sea. Two large oil lamps were suspended from one of the oak beams that supported the low roof.

Jacaud and two other men sat at a table in a corner and played cards. Owen Morgan leaned on the bar beside them, watching the play, a small, greying man with hot Welsh eyes and a face hardened by a lifetime of the sea.

Beside an open window Mallory and Anne faced each other across a small table, smoking cigarettes. Far out to sea the lights of a ship moved slowly across the horizon like something from another world and Anne sighed.

"A big one. I wonder where she's going?"

"Tangiers, the Azores. Take your choice."

"An invitation?"

"Of the most improper kind," he said, and smiled.

"You should do that more often," she said. "It suits you."

Before he could reply a shadow fell across the table. Juliette Vincente was standing there, a half-bottle of champagne and two glasses on her tray. She was perhaps thirty-five, a plain, rather simple-looking woman in a blue woollen dress, thickening slightly at the waist, but her skin was fresh and clean, the cheeks touched with crimson.

"From Monsieur le Comte, madame," she said simply, and placed the bottle and glasses on the table.

At the far end of the bar two or three broad steps lifted to another room where de Beaumont sat beside a pleasant fire. Anne nodded and he raised his glass.

"Small return for a delightful meal."

"Shall I ask him over?" Mallory said.

She shook her head. "Not unless you want to."

A moment or two later the station wagon braked to a halt outside and Raoul Guyon and Fiona got out, turning to help the General. The old man led the way up the steps confidently and entered the bar.

"Over here, Hamish!" Anne called, and he turned and came towards them.

Mallory got to his feet and brought a chair forward and Fiona slipped into the window-seat beside Anne. Guyon picked up the bottle and nodded approvingly.

"Heidsieck, 1952. How typical for the English to reserve the best for themselves. I must really do something to upset the balance."

He moved across to the bar and Hamish Grant produced a brown leather cheroot case and proffered it to Mallory. "Try one of these. Filthy things, but nothing quite like 'em. Picked up the habit in India."

Mallory took one and offered the old man a light as Guyon returned. "Our good friend Owen is raiding his cellar. He can't guarantee that everything will have necessarily come in through the proper channels, but no matter. He tells me that the revenue man only comes once a year and always warns him in advance."

"Understandable," the General said. "They were in the navy together."

Owen Morgan appeared a few moments later and came across with a wide grin. "No need for ice," he said to Guyon as he offered a bottle for inspection. "It's cold enough where that's been."

"Excellent," Guyon said. "I'll open it while you fetch some glasses."

His gaiety was quite infectious and within a few moments he had them all laughing with a description of an outrageous and quite untruthful incident from his past. The conversation which followed moved along spontaneously.

Once or twice Mallory noticed the three men in the corner looking towards them, obviously irritated after some particularly loud burst of laughter from Fiona or Guyon. One of them hammered on the table and called loudly to Owen Morgan for more cognac.

Mallory leaned across to Anne. "The one on the left with the haircut. He was at the wheel of de Beaumont's boat this afternoon. Who is he?"

"They called him Jacaud," she said. "That's all I can tell you. He seems to go everywhere with de Beaumont. I think the others are afraid of him."

"Hardly surprising," Guyon put in. "There's about fifteen stone of bone and muscle there, mostly muscle from the look of him."

Jacaud got to his feet, crossed the bar and mounted the steps to the other room. He leaned on de Beaumont's table and they held a short conversation. Mallory watched them over the rim of his glass. Once, de Beaumont turned and looked towards them. He gazed coolly at Mallory for a moment, then turned back to Jacaud.

The big Frenchman rejoined his friends and Owen Morgan turned on the radio, the sound of music filling the room. Guyon pulled Fiona to her feet and grinned.

"Come on, let's liven the place up a little."

They made an attractive couple as they circled the room. The beautiful young girl on the threshold of womanhood, and Guyon, his lean, sun-blackened face animated and full of life.

Anne Grant watched them wistfully and coloured when she saw that Mallory was looking at her. "Fiona always makes me feel old," she said.

"But not too old." Mallory turned to the General. "You'll excuse us, sir?"

The General touched the champagne bottle lightly and raised his glass. "Enjoy yourselves while you can. I'll make do with this."

They moved into the centre of the floor. She slipped one arm about his neck and danced with her head on his shoulder, her body pressed so closely against him that he could feel the line from breast to thigh.

For a moment, he forgot about everything except the

fact that he was dancing with a warm, exciting girl whose perfume filled his nostrils and caused a pleasant ache of longing in the pit of his stomach.

It had been a long time since he had slept with a woman, but that wasn't the whole explanation. That Anne Grant attracted him was undeniable, but there was something more there, something deeper that for the moment was beyond his comprehension.

The music stopped, a pause between records, and they went back to their table. The others followed a few moments later, and as Fiona seated herself there was a burst of loud laughter from Jacaud and his two friends in the corner, followed by a remark in French, coarse and to the point and quite unprintable.

Guyon swung round, his face hardening. The three men returned his gaze boldly. He took one quick step towards them and Mallory caught him by the sleeve and pulled him down into his chair.

"Let it go."

Guyon was shaking with suppressed anger. "You heard what he said?"

Fiona leaned forward and put a hand on his arm. "Don't let it upset you, Raoul. They've had a little too much to drink, that's all."

A shadow fell across the table and Mallory looked up into the face of the man he had heard Owen Morgan refer to as Marcel a little earlier. He was of medium height and wore denim pants and a blue seaman's jersey. He was very drunk and clutched at the edge of the table to steady himself.

"I think you'd be better off sitting down," Mallory told him in French.

Marcel ignored him, leaned across the table, knocking over a glass, and grabbed Anne by one arm. "You dance with me now?" he mouthed in broken English.

Mallory grabbed for the man's right arm just above the elbow, his thumb hooking into the pressure point. As he swung round, mouth opening in a cry of agony, Guyon kicked him under the right knee-cap. Marcel staggered backwards, lost his balance and sprawled across the other table. Jacaud pushed him to one side, got to his feet and moved forward.

He stood there, swaying slightly as if drunk, and yet the slate-grey eyes were as cold as ice, eternally watchful.

"Two to one, messieurs," he said in excellent English. "You made the odds."

Owen Morgan came round the bar on the run, face very white, eyes blazing. The big Frenchman sent him staggering backwards with a single, contemptuous shove of his hand and laughed harshly.

"He asked for it, Jacaud," de Beaumont called sharply. "Let it end there."

Jacaud ignored him and de Beaumont made no move to come down into the bar, gave no indication of being able or willing to control the situation. He stayed by the fire, a watchful expression on his face.

In that moment Mallory realized that the whole thing had been arranged. That for some reason of his own de Beaumont had deliberately engineered the situation.

Guyon started to rise and Mallory pulled him down again. "My affair."

Jacaud stood there swaying a little, still keeping up the pretence of being drunk, his great hands hooked slightly, every muscle tensed and ready. He lurched forward and stood over them.

"Of course, my friend might be willing to settle for a drink." He nodded at the table. "A bottle of champagne would do."

"Anything to oblige," Mallory said calmly.

He reached for the bottle and, as he turned, reversed his grip and smashed it across the side of the Frenchman's skull. As Anne cried out, Jacaud staggered and fell to one knee. Mallory picked up a chair, moved in fast and smashed it down across the great shoulders. Jacaud grunted, started to heel over and Mallory smashed the broken chair down again and again, until it splintered. He tossed it to one side and waited.

Slowly, painfully, Jacaud reached for the edge of the

bar and pulled himself up. He hung there for a moment, then turned to Mallory, wiping blood from his face casually.

And then, incredibly, he charged, head down like a wounded bull, the great hands reaching out to destroy. Mallory judged his moment exactly, swerved to one side, allowing the Frenchman to plunge past, and slashed him across the kidneys with a *karate* blow delivered with the edge of his hand.

Jacaud screamed and fell to the floor. For a little while he stayed there on his hands and knees, and when he got to his feet he was slobbering like an animal. He lurched forward and Mallory kicked his feet from under him. Jacaud crashed to the floor, rolled over and lay still.

In the silence which followed, de Beaumont came down the steps slowly. He dropped to one knee beside Jacaud, examined him and looked up. "You are a hard man, Colonel Mallory."

"When I have to be," Mallory said. "You could have done something to stop this. Why didn't you?"

He turned without waiting for a reply and went back to the table. "I think that might do for one night. Shall we go?"

Hamish Grant's face was pale, the nostrils flaring slightly as he got to his feet. "You know, I really think it's about time I bought you a drink, Neil. I've got some rather special whiskey back at the house. So Irish that you can taste the peat. I'd like to have your opinion on it."

Anne's face was very white and she was trembling. Mallory squeezed her hand reassuringly and they all walked towards the door. De Beaumont moved to block the way.

"One moment, General. Perhaps I might be allowed to tender my apologies for this distressing affair. At the best of times Jacaud has a short temper. When he's been drinking . . ."

"No need for that, de Beaumont," Hamish Grant said coldly. "I think the matter has been handled quite adequately."

De Beaumont stood there, his smile frozen into place, and then he turned away sharply and they moved outside.

Fiona got behind the wheel, Guyon beside her, and the General and Anne climbed into the back. Mallory slammed the door and leaned in at the open window.

"If you don't mind, General, I'd like to take you up on that drink another time. I've had enough excitement for one night."

As Anne's head turned sharply towards him he turned quickly, giving them no time to argue, and went down the slope towards the jetty. A few moments later the engine coughed into life behind him and the station wagon moved away.

He turned right at the jetty, following a steeply shelving path which brought him down to a strip of sand, white in the moonlight, waves curling in across the shingle with a gentle sucking sound.

He sat on a boulder and lit a cigarette with fingers that trembled slightly. He inhaled deeply, drawing the smoke into his lungs and released it with a long sigh.

Behind him Anne Grant said, "You don't do things by halves, do you?"

"What's the point?" he said simply.

"We seem to have held this conversation before."

When she whispered his name they came together naturally and easily. Her hands pulled his head down as her mouth sought his and her sweetness drove every other thought from his mind. He picked her up in his arms and laid her down gently in the soft sand.

11

❋

In a Lonely Place

THE wind was freshening, lifting the waves into white-caps, and as the dinghy rounded the point water slopped over the gunwale. Guyon carefully eased his weight into the centre and started to bale. He wore a heavy sweater and reefer jacket against the cold. A pair of night-glasses hung around his neck and one of the aquamobiles lay in the prow behind him.

Mallory sat in the stern wearing a black rubber diving suit, the heavy aqualung already strapped into place on his back. As a cross-current started to turn the dinghy in towards the cliffs he opened the throttle on the outboard motor to compensate and glanced at the luminous dial of his watch.

It was 11:45 and there was very little cloud, the sky brilliant with stars, and the moonlight danced across the waves, leaving a trail of silver behind it. The dinghy lifted high on a large swell and swung in towards the great finger of rock which marked the western tip of the island. Mallory opened the throttle again. For a moment the dinghy seemed to stand still and then it forged ahead.

They rounded the point, fighting the cross-currents,

Guyon cursing steadily as water slopped over the sides, and then they were sweeping into calmer water. Beyond, St. Pierre and the Gothic towers of the castle were dark against the sky.

Mallory throttled down again and the dinghy coasted on, the sound of her motor a murmur on the wind. The great reef running between the two islands was deceptively innocent in the moonlight. Waves rolling in from the sea splashed lazily across the rocks, now and then a curtain of white spray lifting into the night like silver lace.

He took the dinghy into the calm waters of the Middle Passage until they reached the first point where the roof closed in and water boiled across great jagged black teeth. He cut the motor and the dinghy slowed and ground gently against a sloping, weed-covered shoulder of rock. Guyon hooked the painter into a crevasse and looked towards St. Pierre through the night-glasses.

"About a quarter of a mile. A long swim."

"Not with the aquamobile," Mallory said.

Guyon got it over the side, the dinghy heeling dangerously. "Rather you than me. The water's like ice. How long will you be?"

Mallory shrugged. "No more than half an hour. I've no intention of hanging around at the other end."

He fitted the rubber mouthpiece between his teeth and adjusted his air supply, touched the knife briefly at his belt and clambered awkwardly over the side on to the reef. He waded into the water, swam to the other side of the dinghy and reached for the aquamobile. Guyon smiled once and Mallory nodded and sank beneath the surface.

Moonlight filtered down through the water, probing into the depths. When he passed beneath the surface of the reef and came into the Middle Passage he entered a darker, more sinister world.

He switched on the powerful spot mounted on top of the scooter and the shaft of light pierced through the darkness in front of him, splaying against the rocks that arched above his head.

He tilted the nose of the aquamobile and went down gently, levelling out at twenty feet. Although his top speed was no more than three knots, he seemed to rush at a terrifying speed into the wall of grey mist that was the edge of his visibility. The great, arched nave of the reef stretched into infinity before him, the water breaking against his mask.

And then he was through and moving into a strange, unreal landscape of jumbled rocks and pale forests of sea-weed waving languidly in the diffused moonlight. He surfaced and looked up at the cliffs of St. Pierre, the pointed towers of the castle dark against the sky.

The moonlight splashed across the face of the cliffs, picking out the dark mouth of the cave. It was now high water and there was no more than a ten- or twelve-foot clearance. Mallory turned the nose of the aquamobile down and levelled out at forty feet. He switched off the spot and moved into a grey phosphorescent mist.

The great fault in the sea-bed dropped beneath him. At least ten fathoms, Anne had said, slicing into the heart of the island. The mist seemed to swing to one side like a curtain, revealing the entrance to the cave, a good sixty feet across as it widened on its way down.

He drifted in, grey-green walls moving past on either side. The water lightened, the grey merging into aqua-marine as artificial light seeped down from the surface. He moved in close to the wall and went forward cautiously.

He stopped abruptly, switching off the aquamobile. From this point on the rough wall of the cave merged into the jetty, great square blocks of masonry like the foundations of some ancient fort descending into the depths. He started up cautiously and immediately the grey-black underbelly of the submarine appeared from the mist.

He had found what he was looking for and to stay any longer was to invite trouble. He turned and flutter-kicked towards the entrance. The light dimmed and he was aware of the current tugging at him.

He swam out into that strange, grey, phosphorescent world and paused to switch on the aquamobile. In that same moment it was torn from his grasp with a metallic clang and a shock-wave, spreading through the water, burst around him.

He turned and saw the frogman suspended in the water about twenty feet away, a weird sea-creature, full of menace, the moonlight glinting on his visor as he reloaded his speargun.

Mallory drove forward, pulling the heavy knife from its sheath. When he was perhaps ten feet away the gun exploded again in a shower of silver bubbles. He swung desperately to one side. The spear hurtled past and he moved in fast, his knife cleaving through rubber and flesh.

The man's body bucked agonizingly, blood rising in a dark cloud as Mallory pulled out the knife and snatched at the air-pipe. As it came free in his hand, air burst out at pressure, bubbles swirling past him on the way to the surface.

He could see the man's face quite clearly now, eyes bulging, teeth clamped together in agony. Quite suddenly he went over backwards in a graceful curve, like a leaf spiralling earthwards in autumn, the weight of his aqualung taking him down.

Mallory struck up towards the surface, chasing his aquamobile, which was rising slowly. He grabbed the handles and switched on, already aware of further shock-waves rippling through the water, bouncing from his body.

The aquamobile surged forward, helped by the turning tide. The sea-bed started to shelve again, and, below, he was aware of the pale forest of seaweed, the ribbons of black rock that were the beginnings of the reef.

Once again he was aware of a shock-wave curling around his body and he glanced to his right. Perhaps fifty yards away and coming up fast through moon-drenched water was a large underwater scooter, at least twice as long as his aquamobile, a frogman trailing behind.

Mallory kicked desperately, urging the aquamobile forward. And then the rocks swarmed up out of the gloom on either side and he rushed into the darkness of the Middle Passage. He switched on his spot, planing down to avoid the overhanging roof. He was aware of a muffled throbbing in his ear, and glanced back. A wide band of diffused light spreading through the mist told him that his pursuer wasn't far behind.

He passed through a section where moonlight streamed in through cracks and fissures in the roof and knew that he was about half-way along the passage, somewhere above the wreck of the freighter. As he came into the clear section he plunged down and at ten fathoms a tapering steel mast loomed out of the gloom. Mallory held on with one hand and waited.

The darkness moved in on him with a terrible, suffocating pressure and the mast seemed to move a little as if the old freighter had rolled. He remembered the dark companionway, dead men's bones crushed under a steel girder, and shivered, suddenly aware of the cold.

He could sense the turbulence in the water, waves rippling down. When he looked up there was the weird, incandescent glow of the spot-lamp on the other scooter as it passed overhead. He waited for a moment or two, then went up slowly.

At twenty feet he levelled out, switched on the motor, but not the spot, and went after the other scooter. Only in patches was visibility really bad and at this depth the moonlight streamed in through fissures in the rock like regularly spaced lamps along a dark road.

When he emerged at last from the great central nave into clear water he switched off the aquamobile and surfaced.

Raoul Guyon sat in the stern of the dinghy. A yard or two away the frogman stood waist-deep in water on the shelving reef beside his scooter, a loaded spear-gun in his hands. It was almost as if they were holding a conversation.

Mallory released his grip on the aquamobile, went under the surface and swam forward. He erupted in a surge of power, slid his right arm about the man's neck and fell backwards, towing him into deep water, tearing the airhose from his mouth.

They sank down through the clear water, the spear-gun spiralling off to one side. Mallory wrenched again with his free hand, pulling away the mask, and the man's face turned up, contorted with fear.

Mallory hung on, even when a clutching hand reached backwards, wrenching away his own air-hose. He compressed his lips and tightened his grip. Blood began to seep from the man's nostrils in two clouds and a moment later he swung loosely against Mallory's arm. Mallory unlocked his fingers and the body bounced away, spun round twice and started to sink.

There was a roaring in his ears and his temples pounded. He kicked for the surface and bumped against the side of the dinghy, gasping and choking for breath. Guyon reached over and grasped his outstretched hand and Mallory stumbled up the sloping shelf of rock and crouched on his hands and knees, chest heaving.

Guyon jumped knee-deep into the water beside him and helped him up, pulling away the mask, his face strained and anxious in the moonlight. When he spoke his voice sounded faint and far away and Mallory shook his head several times.

The roaring subsided abruptly and he gasped: "No time for questions. I ran into a little trouble. We'd better get moving."

"You found *L'Alouette?*"

"She's there, all right. Moored to the jetty under the island just like we thought. Room for a couple more from the look of the place."

He unbuckled the heavy aqualung, swung it into the prow and clambered aboard the dinghy. As he started the outboard motor Guyon unhooked the painter and followed him. A second later and the dinghy was moving back towards Île de Roc, following the twisting channel between the great rocks which already reared up on either side as the tide turned.

"What happens now?" Guyon said.

"We call up Leviathan the moment we get back. Those motor torpedo boats from St. Helier will be here before you know it."

The dinghy rocked in the turbulence as it swept on a fast current between high black walls and turned towards the point. Behind them a full-throated roar shattered the night and Guyon raised the night-glasses and looked back. When he took them down his face looked very white in the moonlight.

"It's that damned speedboat of de Beaumont's. Coming up fast on this side of the reef. Must be doing all of fifteen knots."

Mallory glanced back, catching a brief glimpse of the thin pencil of light that was the speedboat's spot, and opened the throttle of the dinghy's outboard motor. The strong current was running against them now as they tried to breast the point, and the light craft was twisted round, a wave splashing across her prow.

"Throw the aqualung overboard," Mallory shouted.

Guyon scrambled to his knees, reached for the straps, heaved and slid the aqualung over. There was an immediate difference, the prow riding over the next wave, and they turned the point and moved into what should have been calmer water.

The turning tide at this point clashed headlong with the usual strong coastal current, and all around them great patches of white water joined with others, sending irregular waves cascading against the cliffs, the undertow sucking them out again.

The dinghy wallowed in the trough between two great swells, her speed cut in half, and, behind, the roar of the speedboat drew inexorably nearer.

"We'll never make it to the harbour," Guyon called. "A couple more minutes and they'll see us."

A great heaving swell was building up to starboard. As it swept in, lifting the dinghy high into the air, Mallory caught a glimpse of Hamish Grant's house tucked into a fold at the top of the cliffs, a light shining in one of the ground-floor rooms. He swung the tiller over and the current drove the dinghy in towards the cliffs at tremendous speed.

The gap in the inlet had been at least twenty yards across, but the real problem was that line of jagged rocks blocking the entrance as surely as if it had been a steel portcullis. The one slim hope was that the waves, sweeping in, would raise the water-level and carry them over.

He shouted to Guyon: "This is going to be rough. Hang on and get ready to swim."

The Frenchman looked back once, his lips moving in reply, but the roaring of the sea drowned his words. Mallory held on to the tiller with both hands. Strange, swirling currents twisted them round and the dinghy was carried helplessly in.

The opening of the cove appeared suddenly in the face of the cliff, water boiling through in a great surge. At one side white spray foamed high in the air, while, all around, dirty cream patches formed as rocks showed through.

The dinghy slewed broadside into the entrance, lifted high and smashed down upon a great green slab of rock. The tiller was wrenched from Mallory's hand and the outboard motor was torn away with a section of the stern.

The dinghy slithered forward across the reef and ground to a halt, a jagged edge of rock smashing through the hull. Guyon went head first over the prow with a cry and Mallory went after him.

The Frenchman tried to stand and Mallory plunged through the boiling surf, hands outstretched to meet him. For a moment they clung together and then another wave, cascading in across the reef, bowled them over.

Guyon went under, and Mallory, striking after him, found himself in deep water. He grabbed the Frenchman by the collar of his jacket and struck out, the current pushing them forward. His feet touched sand and he stood up, pulling Guyon after him. Water boiled waist-high again, tugging at their limbs. As it receded they lurched forward, feet slipping in the shingle, and staggered up the narrow strip of beach at the base of the cliffs.

Someone was playing the piano, an old, pre-war Cole Porter number with something of the night in it, something of warmth and love and hope that seemed to belong to another age than this.

Crouching in the bushes below the terrace, Mallory was caught for a brief moment, unable to go forward or back. Guyon groaned beside him, coughing up water, and

Mallory pulled him to his feet and they staggered up the steps.

The french window was ajar, one end of a red velvet curtain billowing out as a gust of wind lifted it. He took a deep breath and opened it wide.

The fire burned brightly on the stone hearth and Hamish Grant's hair gleamed like silver in the lamplight as he leaned in his wing-backed chair, smoking a cheroot. Anne sat opposite, staring into the fire while Fiona played the piano.

It was Fiona who saw them first. She gave a sudden gasp, her hands striking a false chord, and jumped to her feet. Anne stood up slowly and Hamish Grant turned his head and looked directly at the window.

"Sorry about this," Mallory said as he moved forward, one arm still around Guyon's shoulders.

Guyon retched suddenly and started to cough again. Mallory helped him to a chair by the fire and the Frenchman fell into it with a groan.

Anne stayed surprisingly calm. "Brandy, Fiona," she said. "Quickly. Two glasses."

Mallory moved forward, water streaming from his rubber suit, and stretched out his hands to the fire, shivering involuntarily as the warmth enveloped him. Hamish Grant reached out to the dark figure, dimly seen, and touched the wet rubber suit.

"A strange time to go swimming."

"Under the circumstances we didn't have much choice." Mallory turned to Anne, who gazed up at him searchingly. "You're on the phone here, aren't you?"

She nodded. "Linked to Guernsey by cable, but it hasn't been working since yesterday's storm. That often happens. There's the radio telephone on *Foxhunter,* of course. Is it important?"

"You could say that." Mallory turned to Guyon, who was gulping the brandy Fiona had passed to him. "I'll have to get down to the harbour straight away. I can use the transmitter."

"We'll both go," Guyon said. "There could be trouble waiting down there."

"Any chance of an explanation?" Hamish Grant enquired mildly.

Mallory took the glass of brandy Fiona offered, swallowed half of it down and coughed as the fiery liquor caught at the back of his throat. "I'd say you were entitled to one under the circumstances. I was sent here by British Intelligence and Captain Guyon by the same branch on the other side of the Channel. We were asked to do a quick check on de Beaumont."

"I see," Hamish Grant said. "I take it he's up to no good?"

"Very much so. His present activities are a direct threat to the interests of his own government and the fact that he's seen fit to operate from British territory presents a serious complication. On top of that, we don't like what he's doing anyway."

Hamish Grant smiled faintly. "How strange. Two great nations side by side through the centuries. We have our quarrels, but somehow they're always in the family. The moment the chips are down we move in to help each other so fast it's almost frightening."

"Can I ask what happened to Van Sondergard?" Anne asked.

"I paid him double what you would have done and shipped him out."

"And the incident on the wharf? That was arranged, too?"

He nodded. "It got a little out of hand. That's why I had to get so rough. I'm sorry."

"I'm not," she said simply.

He reached out and touched her face and something glowed deep in her eyes. Her hand went up, holding his against her cheek, and she turned her head, touching her lips to his cold palm. For a brief moment it was as if they were alone. As if the others had ceased to exist. It was Hamish Grant who broke the spell.

"I should imagine dry clothes should be the first step and you'll need the car."

"I'll get it out of the garage," Fiona said quickly.

She was standing at the side of Guyon's chair. She

smiled down at him, then went out through the french windows. Guyon got to his feet and he and Mallory followed Anne out of the room, leaving a trail of sea-water across the carpet.

She found dry socks, some old service slacks and a couple of heavy sweaters from Hamish Grant's wardrobe and left the two men in his room to change. When they went downstairs ten minutes later Jagbir was pouring coffee into cups arranged on a table beside the fire. Hamish Grant still sat in his chair, but there was no sign of the girls.

The little Gurkha offered them coffee, no visible excitement on his face, and the old man said: "There was a mention of possible trouble when you go down to the harbour. The violent sort, I presume. Are you armed?"

Guyon answered: "I had a revolver in the pocket of my reefer coat. I lost it coming through the surf."

"You'll find another in the top right-hand drawer of the desk behind you," the old man said. "Half a box of cartridges somewhere at the back. There should be a Lüger there as well, but that's already loaded."

Guyon opened the drawer and came back, the revolver in one hand, the Lüger in the other. "You can have the Lüger," the old man went on. "I'll keep the Webley myself, if you don't mind."

Guyon slipped the Lüger into his pocket and started to load the Webley. Anne and Fiona came in. They were both wearing heavy sheepskin coats and Anne was binding a scarf about her head, peasant-fashion.

She smiled at Mallory. "Ready when you are."

He shook his head gently. "Not on your life. You stay right here."

A slight crease appeared between her eyes and Fiona started to protest. Hamish Grant cut in sharply, "They'll have enough to worry about without you two."

Fiona turned to Anne, but her sister-in-law sighed and shook her head. "He's right, Fiona. We'd only be in the way." She smiled up at Mallory. "So we sit and wait? How long for?"

"With any luck the whole thing should be wrapped up

into a neat parcel by breakfast. And, I warn you, I'll have an appetite."

"I'll hold you to that."

He touched her hand briefly and led the way out into the hall. The shooting brake was parked at the bottom of the steps, its engine ticking over, and he climbed behind the wheel and waited for Guyon. The young Frenchman was standing at the top of the steps with Fiona, Anne in the doorway behind them. The young girl reached up, kissed him and hurried inside. He came down the steps and got into the passenger seat, his face grim.

Mallory drove away quickly, turning out through the gates along the white road and down the hill towards the harbour. The hotel was in darkness and the cove was exactly as they had left it, *Foxhunter* moored to one side of the jetty, Guyon's hired launch on the other.

Mallory braked to a halt at the end of the jetty, switched off the engine and got out. Moonlight silvered the water and the night sky was like a warm dark velvet cushion scattered with diamonds.

"So far, so good," he said to Guyon, and led the way along the jetty.

He jumped to *Foxhunter*'s deck and went into the wheelhouse. He switched on the light and cursed softly. The radio telephone had been wrenched from its fastening on the far wall and lay in the corner, smashed beyond repair, a fire-axe beside it.

"They beat us to it after all."

He pushed past Guyon, hurried down the companionway and through the saloon to the aft cabin. He dropped to one knee, opened the locker beneath his bunk and rummaged inside.

"Is this what you are looking for, Colonel Mallory?" Raoul Guyon said softly.

Mallory got to his feet and turned. Guyon stood on the other side of the table, a drawer open, holding the small electronic transmitter that was Mallory's only link with the department.

"Good man," Mallory said, and took a step forward.

Guyon dropped the set to the floor and ground his

heel into it twice, at the same time taking the Lüger from his coat pocket.

Mallory stood staring at him, a slight frown on his face, and a voice said: "Excellent, Captain Guyon. I was really beginning to despair of you."

As Mallory turned, de Beaumont stepped out of the shadows of the dark galley, Jacaud at his side, a submachine-gun in his hands.

12

•

To the Dark Tower

THEY were close to the island now and Marcel cut the engine to half-speed and took *Foxhunter* in slowly towards the dark arch. The speedboat bobbed behind them on a long towline and as Mallory looked out to sea a shadow moved in from the horizon, blanketing the stars.

Guyon stood by the rail a few feet away talking to de Beaumont in a low voice and Jacaud leaned against the wheelhouse, the sub-machine-gun in his hands. One of his eyes was half closed, the right side of his face swollen and disfigured by a huge purple bruise, and his eyes stared at Mallory unwinkingly.

They moved into the dark entrance and Mallory shivered, chilled by the damp air, and then they were through. From end to end the cave was about a hundred yards long and perhaps fifty feet across. Beneath the surface, as he had discovered earlier, it was even wider.

The long stone jetty was brightly illuminated by two arc-lamps and they coasted in to tie up behind a magnificent forty-foot, steel-hulled motor-yacht, the name *Fleur de Lys* painted across her counter.

The submarine was moored on the far side, squat and

black in the water, and looked even smaller than Mallory had imagined. A dozen or so men in the uniform of the French Navy worked busily, loading stores on board under the supervision of a slim, rather boyish-looking lieutenant in peaked cap and reefer jacket. As they went up the short ladder to the jetty, he came forward, saluting de Beaumont casually.

"How are things going, Fenelon?" de Beaumont asked. "Any snags?"

Fenelon shook his head. "We'll be ready on schedule."

"Good, I'll give you a final briefing at 9 a.m." Fenelon went back to his men and de Beaumont turned to Mallory. "Magnificent, isn't she? And just the thing for our purposes. Small, compact—only needs a crew of sixteen. You're familiar with the type?"

"Only on paper."

"This one has quite a history. Built at Deutsche Werft in 1945 and sunk with all hands within a month of commissioning. After she was raised she was transferred to the French."

"And now she's yours," Mallory said. "A chequered career."

A body was against the far wall, covered by a tarpaulin, webbed feet turned to one side, blood streaking the pool of sea-water in which it lay.

"We couldn't find the other one. The current must have taken him under the reef." De Beaumont shook his head. "A nasty way to die."

The words seemed to carry an implicit threat, but Mallory refused to be drawn, and de Beaumont smiled faintly and led the way across to where a flight of stone steps lifted a hundred feet into the gloom, curving round one wall of the cave. They mounted the steps and emerged on to a stone landing, and de Beaumont led the way to the far end of a passage, passing several doors. One or two stood open to show narrow service bunks and grey blankets neatly folded. From a side entrance there came the smell of cooking.

He opened another door and they entered a large hall, great curved beams of oak arching into the gloom. There was a wide marble staircase and, above it, a gallery. At one side logs blazed in an immense medieval fireplace.

"Quite a sight, isn't it? The money these Victorian industrialists must have had to throw around, and every stone brought in by boat."

His tone was casual, mannered. He might have been a rather complacent host showing a friend over his new place. They went up the great staircase and moved along the gallery to the far end. De Beaumont opened a door to disclose a narrow spiral staircase. At intervals there were slotted windows and Mallory could see far out to sea as they mounted higher and higher.

They reached a stone landing and paused outside a door. De Beaumont went in, leaving it ajar. The room contained a great deal of radio equipment and an operator sat before a transmitting set, headphones clamped to his ears. He stood up when de Beaumont appeared. There was a murmur of conversation and then the Colonel came back outside.

He continued up the spiral staircase, Mallory, Guyon and Marcel following behind, Jacaud bringing up the rear. At last they emerged on a small landing and de Beaumont opened his final door.

The room was circular in shape and quite large. It was comfortably furnished, Persian carpets covering the floor, logs burning brightly in the wide fireplace. The walls were lined with books except for a section perhaps twenty feet long covered by a velvet curtain. De Beaumont pulled it to one side, revealing a curved glass window.

"One of my little improvements. On a clear day you can see France." He indicated a chair by the fire. "If you please."

Mallory sat in the chair and Jacaud moved to stand behind him, the sub-machine-gun held ready. Marcel stood by the window, a revolver in his right hand held against his thigh. Guyon remained by the door and Mallory looked across at him. Guyon returned his gaze calmly, giving nothing away, and Mallory turned to de Beaumont, who was now sitting in the opposite chair.

"I will not insult your intelligence by fencing with

you, Colonel Mallory," he said. "For some time I was a prisoner of the Viets in Indo-China. There is little they failed to teach me at first hand about the extraction of information from the unco-operative. Jacaud was senior warrant officer of my regiment. He shared my experiences. I need hardly add that he would welcome an opportunity to experiment."

"No need to go on," Mallory said. "I get the point."

"Excellent," de Beaumont said. "We can get down to business. As you may now have deduced for yourself, Captain Guyon is something of a double agent. When the *Deuxième* offered him employment they were not aware that he was already a loyal member of the O.A.S. A most convenient arrangement. He confirms the fact that the *Bureau* had no real grounds for suspecting *L'Alouette* to be in hiding here. That his assignment to Île de Roc to work with you was at the request of British Intelligence. I'd like to know why."

"We had a man here watching you," Mallory said. "Just routine, because of who you are and what you are. He drifted in on the tide the other evening. Accidental drowning was the coroner's verdict."

"He had a habit of taking long walks on the cliffs after dark with a pair of night-glasses," de Beaumont said. "Rather dangerous. Someone should have warned him."

"You made a mistake there," Mallory said. "To my chief it meant only one thing. Our man had seen something important. With the French combing every creek and inlet on their side of the Channel it gave him a rather nasty feeling to think that she might be sitting it out in the Channel Islands."

"A pity," de Beaumont said. "Now I must move out rather sooner than I had intended. On the other hand, neither my immediate nor long-term plans will be affected in the slightest." He stood up and smiled politely. "Under happier circumstances I should have enjoyed talking to you. We must have a great deal in common. I'm sure you'll understand that my time is limited."

"Naturally," Mallory said ironically and got to his feet.

He had often wondered about this moment, how it would come and when. The strange thing was that he was not afraid. More curious than anything else. Jacaud moved restlessly behind him and Marcel came away from the wall, the gun still held against his leg.

De Beaumont took a revolver from his pocket, crossed to Guyon and handed it to him. "Will you do the honours, Captain? A soldier's end, I think."

Guyon's hand tightened on the butt of the revolver and he looked across at Mallory, his face very white. Quite suddenly he grabbed de Beaumont by the front of his coat, pulling him forward, and rammed the barrel of the revolver against his throat.

There was a moment of stillness and then de Beaumont laughed gently. "You know, our friends in Paris have been worried about you for some time now, Guyon. I can understand why. You're slipping. I should have thought an officer of your experience would have been able to tell the difference in weight between a revolver loaded with blanks and one loaded with live ammunition."

He reached up and took the revolver from Guyon's hand and Guyon looked across at Mallory and smiled wryly. "Sometimes we can be too clever, my friend."

"Nice to have you back," Mallory said.

De Beaumont opened the door and nodded to Marcel. "Take him below and watch him carefully. I'll send Colonel Mallory down later."

He closed the door behind them, turned to Mallory and smiled. "And now that we all know exactly where we are we can perhaps relax for half an hour." He took a bottle and two glasses from a cupboard in the corner and returned to his chair. "This is really quite an excellent cognac. I think you'll enjoy it."

Mallory sat in the opposite chair, aware of Jacaud at his back, and waited for what was to come. He accepted a glass of cognac, drank a little and leaned back. "I can't understand what you hope to gain from all this. Murder and assassination will only lose you what little support you command."

"A matter of opinion," de Beaumont said. "The only

politics which seem to matter in this modern world are the politics of violence. Palestine, Cyprus and Algeria were all examples of victory achieved by a deliberate and carefully planned use of violence and assassination. We can do the same."

"The circumstances are completely different. In the cases you've quoted, nationalistic elements were opposed to a colonial power. In your own, Frenchmen are murdering Frenchmen."

"They are not worthy of the name, the swine we have dealt with so far. Loud-mouths, professional liberals and scheming politicians who feathered their own nests while I and men like me rotted in the Viet prison camps." De Beaumont laughed bitterly. "I remember our homecoming only too well. Booed all the way into Marseilles by Communist dock workers."

"Ancient history," Mallory said. "Nobody wants to know. In any case, unless they'd been through the same experience themselves they wouldn't know what you're talking about."

"But you have," de Beaumont said. "Deep inside, I think you know what I mean. You learned a hard lesson from the Chinese. You put it down in cold print in that book of yours. What happened when you put it into practice?"

He stared into the fire, a frown on his face. "It was going to be different in Algeria, we were certain of that. We fought the *fells* in the *jebel* of the Atlas Mountains, in the heat of the Sahara, in the alleys of Algiers, and we were beating them. In the end we had them by the throat."

He turned to Mallory. "I was in the army plot of the 13th May 1958. They gave us no choice. They would have arrested my friends and me, tried us on trumped-up atrocity charges, designed to please the loud-mouths and fellow-travellers back home in Paris. We put de Gaulle in power because we believed in the ideal of a French Algeria, a greater France."

"And once he was in control he did exactly the opposite to what you had intended," Mallory said. "One of the great ironies of post-war history."

De Beaumont swallowed some more cognac and continued. "Even more ironic that I, Phillipe de Beaumont, descendant of one of the greatest of French military families, should have helped place in power the man who has destroyed the greatness of his country."

"That remains to be seen," Mallory said. "I'd say that Charles de Gaulle was moved by one thing only—deep patriotism. Whatever he's done he's done because he thought it best for France."

De Beaumont shrugged. "So we disagree? It's of little moment. After his visit to St. Malo on the 3rd of next month he will no longer present a problem."

"I don't know what you have in mind, but I wouldn't count on anything. How many times have your people failed now? Eight, isn't it?"

"I flatter myself that my own organization has been rather more successful. These affairs need the trained mind, Mallory. Everything I handle is a military operation. *L'Alouette* affair, I have handled personally from the beginning. My colleagues in Paris know nothing about it. I work strictly on my own and use them as an information service only."

Mallory shook his head. "You can't last much longer. You're working on too big a scale. Already *L'Alouette*'s becoming more of a liability than anything else."

"You couldn't be more wrong." De Beaumont got to his feet, took a couple of charts from the cupboard beside his chair and crossed to a small table. "Come over here. You'll find this interesting."

They were Admiralty charts of the area between Guernsey and the French coast and he joined them together quickly. "Here is Île de Roc and St. Pierre, thirty miles south-west of Guernsey. The nearest French soil is Pointe du Château, only twenty miles away. You know the area?"

Mallory shook his head. "The closest I've been is Brest."

"A dangerous coast of small islands and reefs, lonely and wild. You will notice Île de Monte only a quarter of a mile off the coast, the Gironde Marshes opposite. There is a small cottage on an island perhaps half a mile into the marsh on the main creek. Eight miles from a road and very lonely. Not even a telephone. There are only two people in residence at the moment."

"And you want them?"

"Only the man. Henri Granville."

Mallory straightened, a frown on his face. "You mean Granville the judge, the Procureur Général who retired last month?"

"I congratulate you on your intimate knowledge of French affairs. He arrived there with his wife yesterday. They are quite alone. Of course, no one is supposed to know. He's fond of solitude—solitude and birds. Unfortunately for him, a contact of mine in Paris got news of his movements last night and let me know at once. I'm sending Jacaud across in *L'Alouette* later today. His execution should cause quite a stir."

"You're crazy," Mallory said. "He must be eighty if he's a day. On top of that, he's one of the best-loved men in France. God in heaven, everybody loves Granville! Politics doesn't enter into it."

"On three occasions now he has presided at tribunals which have condemned old comrades of mine to death," de Beaumont said. "Now he must pay the consequences. By striking at Granville we prove once and for all that we are a force to be reckoned with. That no man, however powerful, no matter what his public standing, is safe from our vengeance."

"Henri Granville never condemned anyone in his life without good reason. Harm him in any way and you'll bring the mountain in on you." Mallory shook his head. "You'll never get away with it."

De Beaumont smiled faintly, crossed to the fire and poured more cognac into his glass. "You think not?" He swallowed a little of the cognac and sighed. "I will postpone your execution till this evening. By that time Jacaud will have returned. It will give me some satisfaction in sending you to your death with the knowledge that Henri Granville has preceded you."

"Which remains to be seen," Mallory said.

De Beaumont turned and indicated a tattered battle

standard hanging above the fireplace. "An ancestor of mine carried that himself at Waterloo when his standard-bearer was shot. It was with me at Dien-Bien-Phu. I managed to hang on to it during all those bitter months of captivity. You will notice it bears the motto of the de Beaumonts."

" 'Who dares, wins'," Mallory said.

"I would remember that if I were you."

"Something you seem to have forgotten," Mallory said. "When that ancestor of yours picked up that standard at Waterloo he didn't carry it forward on his own. There was a regiment of guards backing him up all the way and I seem to remember that at Dien-Bien-Phu you commanded a regiment of colonial paratroops. But, then, that's France I'm speaking about. The real France. Something you wouldn't know anything about."

For a moment something glowed in de Beaumont's eyes, but he pushed back his anger and forced a smile. "Take him below, Jacaud. He and Guyon can spend their last hours together trying to solve an impossible problem. The thought will amuse me."

Jacaud gave Mallory a push towards the door. As he opened it, de Beaumont said calmly: "And, Jacaud, when I next see Colonel Mallory I expect him to be in his present condition. You understand?"

Jacaud turned sharply, a growl rising in his throat. For a moment he seemed about to defy de Beaumont and then he turned suddenly and pushed Mallory forward.

They went down the spiral staircase, Mallory leading, all the time aware of the machine-gun at his back. The gallery was in half-darkness, the fire a heap of glowing ashes, as they crossed the hall and went through the door which led to the living-quarters and the cave.

At the end of a long whitewashed corridor they found Marcel sitting on a chair outside a door, reading a newspaper, the revolver stuck in his belt.

He looked up at Jacaud, eyes raised enquiringly. "When?"

"This evening when I get back from the mainland."

Jacaud turned to Mallory and patted the sub-machine-gun. A red glow seemed to light up behind the cold eyes. "Personally, Colonel Mallory."

Mallory moved into the cell. As the door clanged behind him, Guyon swung his legs to the floor and sat looking at him.

He grinned suddenly. "You wouldn't by any chance have such a thing as a cigarette on you, would you?"

13

●

Council of War

"I HAD lost all belief or interest in right or wrong. In the end you believe only in your friends, the comrade who had his throat cut the previous night. That was what six years in Algeria had done for me."

Raoul Guyon stood by the small barred window gazing into the night. When he turned he looked tired.

"And this is why you joined the O.A.S.?" Mallory said.

Guyon shook his head. "I was in Algiers in 1958. So much blood that I was sickened by it. There was a young Moorish girl. For a little while we tried to shelter from the storm together. They found her on the beach one morning, stripped, mutilated. I had to identify the body. The following day I was badly wounded and sent back to France to convalesce. When I returned my comrades seemed to have the only solution. To bring back de Gaulle."

"You took part in the original plot?"

Guyon shrugged. "I was on the fringe. Just one more junior officer. But to me de Gaulle stood for order out of chaos. Afterwards most of us were posted to other units. I spent five months on patrol with the Camel Corps in the Hoggar."

"And did you find what you were looking for?"

"Almost," Guyon said. "There was a day of heat and thirst when I almost had it, when the rocks shimmered and the mountains danced in a blue haze and I was a part of it. Almost, but not quite."

"What happened after that?"

"I was posted back to Algeria to one of the worst districts. A place of barbed wire and fear, where violence erupted like a disease and life was no longer even an act of faith. I was wounded again last year just before General Challe's abortive coup. Not seriously, but enough to give me a legitimate excuse to put in a request to be placed on unpaid leave. The night before I left, Legrande visited me in my hotel room. Offered me work with the *Deuxième Bureau*."

"And you accepted?"

"In a strange way it offered me some sort of escape. Later, in Paris, I was approached by O.A.S. agents. As an ex-paratroop officer and supporter of the original coup which had placed de Gaulle in power, I must have seemed an obvious choice."

"And you informed Legrande?"

"As soon as I could get in touch with him. That was the funny thing. I didn't even have to make a choice. It was almost as if it had been made for me. He told me to accept the offer. From his point of view an agent with contacts in that direction would obviously be valuable."

"And yet we were informed that the *Deuxième* had no real suspicions about de Beaumont. Surely you must have had some sort of a lead on him through your Paris connections with the other side?"

"Not really. I was only on the edge of their organization. De Beaumont's name was mentioned as one sympathetic to their aims. On the other hand, his political opinions are well known in France. There was certainly never any hint that he might be an active worker."

"And all this time you were completely accepted?"

"I certainly thought so. As a new recruit to the *Deuxième,* it was obvious that my sources would be limited, but I passed on selected information on Legrande's orders. I certainly never managed to get close to any of the really big men, but I was working towards it. On two occasions he even allowed me to warn some of the lesser fry when their arrest was imminent."

"What about *L'Alouette?*"

"That was the thing which puzzled us from the beginning. The complete absence of information as to her whereabouts, even in O.A.S. circles. Because of that Legrande told me to inform my Paris contacts that I had been assigned to the Channel Islands merely to run a routine check on de Beaumont, just to make sure that he was behaving himself. Legrande felt that at least it would prove once and for all whether a definite link existed."

"Something he didn't see fit to inform us at our end."

"I'm sorry about that, but Legrande never lives in the present—only the future. He envisaged a possible situation in which my other activities could prove useful. Under the circumstances it seemed wiser to present myself as Raoul Guyon, an accredited agent of the *Bureau* and nothing more."

"I see the old fox is still a believer in playing his cards as they fall," Mallory said. "It shows in his poker game."

"A remark strangely similar to one he made about you just before I left."

Mallory grinned. "One thing at least has come out of all this. De Beaumont definitely does have a link with the O.A.S. in Paris because he was warned that you were coming. The one thing I don't understand is why he didn't think it strange that you hadn't told them about *L'Alouette* affair."

"The first thing he asked me coming across on the boat. A difficult question to answer."

"And how did you?"

"Told him the *Bureau* believed the whole business to be the work of an independent group. That this was confirmed for me personally by the obvious ignorance of the affair in O.A.S. circles. That as an ex-paratroop officer who had taken part in the coup of June '58, only to be betrayed by de Gaulle, I would much prefer to work with him."

"And he accepted that?"

"He seemed to at the time."

"It all sounds pretty shaky to me."

"It obviously did to de Beaumont." Guyon grinned wryly. "On the other hand, I didn't have time to think up anything better and I did make my own move against you just before they did, remember?"

"That was quick thinking."

The young Frenchman shrugged. "When I saw what they had done to the radio telephone it seemed logical to assume they were still on board, that we were under observation. It seemed wise to establish my credentials while I still could and I remembered seeing you put the transmitter in the table drawer earlier in the afternoon."

"And you'd never met him previously?"

Guyon shook his head. "As I told you before, only as one of a crowd. Naturally, I knew a great deal about him. He was one of the really great paratroop officers, you know."

"I've been going over everything he said to me upstairs," Mallory said. "None of it really makes sense. In the end he must lose. The murder of a fine old man like Henri Granville on its own will be sufficient to lose him, and those who think like him, a great deal of sympathy, and yet he goes on. I wonder why?"

"He was always a strange, ascetic man. A cross between religious fanatic and soldier. The surrender at Dien-Bien-Phu, the humiliation of the Viet camps and our subsequent withdrawal from Indo-China were a source of lasting shame to him. Like many of his kind, he swore it would never happen again."

"And in spite of everything he could do it did."

Guyon nodded. "De Beaumont is the last of one of our most noble families, his only heir a brother who is a professor of political history at the Sorbonne. A man with pronounced left-wing sympathies. One of his ancestors was one of the few nobles to give wholehearted support to the revolution in 1789, another was a general under Napoleon. For one hundred and fifty years the de Beaumonts have been one of the greatest of French families."

"Something of a national calamity if he had to be arrested."

"Exactly. The government was more than happy when he chose to reside in the Channel Islands. At the time it seemed to dispose of him as an immediate problem."

"Which he has now become," Mallory said, "and in more ways than one."

"You are thinking of his threat to dispose of de Gaulle during his visit to St. Malo next month?" Guyon shook his head, lay on the other bed, pillowing his head on his hands. "I'm not too worried about that. They won't get de Gaulle. He's indestructible, that one. Like one of those rocks out there on the reef after a storm. A little more weathered, but still standing."

"Which leaves us with the Granville affair," Mallory said. "And the hell of it is there doesn't seem to be a damned thing we can do about it."

He lit a cigarette and lay on his back, gazing at the ceiling, going over the events of the previous couple of hours in his mind. After a while he said softly: "The first rule in this game is that the job must come before everything else. Most men I've worked with, in your position, would have played along with de Beaumont, would even have executed me if necessary."

"Perhaps I saw the situation differently," Guyon said.

"You moved so fast you didn't even notice the difference in weight the blanks made. Why?"

"Something I've been asking myself on and off for the past hour or more. It's not easy to explain. Let's just say that suddenly people have become important to me again and leave it at that."

He turned his face to the wall and Mallory lay there, smoking his cigarette, thinking how strange it was that a young man, all feeling burned out of him by the flames of two savage wars, should be brought back to life by that oldest and most elemental of human emotions—love.

He was cold and stiff and his limbs ached. He pulled the blanket over his legs and checked his watch. It was almost 5 a.m. and he lay in the darkness listening to the rain and the wind. After a while he drifted into sleep again.

He became aware that someone was prodding him and opened his eyes. Raoul Guyon squatted beside him. Grey light seeped into the room through the barred window and Mallory swung his legs to the floor.

"Still raining?"

Guyon nodded. "Hasn't let up all night. It's almost eight."

Mallory walked to the door and peered through the iron grille into the corridor outside. A young sailor sat in a chair reading a book, a heavy service revolver in the holster at his waist.

Mallory crossed to the window. The casement opened easily enough, but the bars set in the ledge on either side were strong and firm. He looked into the grey morning, out along the reef to Île de Roc. Rain slanted down and visibility was poor, a cold mist drifting close to the surface of the water.

"I wonder what they're doing over there?" Guyon said at his shoulder.

"They must have realized by now that something's gone wrong." Mallory shrugged. "If they've any sense at all they'll have brought in Owen Morgan and gone to Guernsey for help in your launch."

"Surely de Beaumont will have considered that possibility?"

"He probably has. That's what's worrying me."

There was a rattle of bolts and the door opened. As they both turned, Marcel entered and stood to one side, a revolver in his right hand. The young sailor followed, carrying a tray which he placed on the bed. They withdrew without saying a word, bolting the door again.

The food was simple, bread and cheese and hot coffee,

and Mallory suddenly realized how hungry he was. They sat on either side of the tray to eat and finished off by sharing his last cigarette.

Afterwards he lay on the bed waiting for something to happen, while Guyon paced restlessly up and down the cell, the rain hammering against the window. It was almost ten o'clock when the door opened again and de Beaumont entered, Marcel at his back.

He seemed in a good humour and smiled cheerfully. "Good morning, gentlemen. I trust you spent a good night? Your quarters are adequate?"

"I've seen worse," Mallory admitted.

"Anything I can get you?"

"The condemned man's last wish?" Mallory shrugged. "We could do with some cigarettes. That's about all."

Marcel took a packet of Gauloise from his pocket and threw them on the bed. "Anything else?" de Beaumont said politely.

Mallory put a cigarette in his mouth and tossed the packet to Guyon. "I don't think so."

"Then you will excuse me? You'll be interested to know that Jacaud and his men left for Pointe du Château fifteen minutes ago as scheduled. Under the circumstances I think it's time I paid a visit to our friends on Île de Roc."

"I wouldn't count on anyone being there to meet you."

"Oh, they'll be there, all right. I can assure you of that."

De Beaumont smiled faintly as if enjoying some private joke, nodded to Marcel and passed outside. The door closed and the bolts were rammed home with a harsh finality. Guyon turned with a gesture of despair and Mallory motioned him to silence. When he went to the door the young sailor was back on his chair reading a magazine.

Mallory crossed to the window and looked outside. A minute or two later he heard the sound of an engine and *Foxhunter* came into view, running alongside the reef towards Île de Roc.

"There he goes."

Guyon moved to the window, peered out, and frowned. "But why has he taken *Foxhunter*?"

"Easier to handle than *Fleur de Lys* on the short run and there's too much sea for the speedboat."

Guyon, thinking of Fiona, dropped his cigarette and stamped on it viciously. "I didn't like his last remark. He sounded far too sure of himself. As if he knew for certain that the General and the girls would still be on the island."

"I imagine he does," Mallory said. "It's been a long night. He could have been up to anything, but that isn't important at the moment. He probably only intends to bring them back here for safe custody until he's ready to move out."

"You may be right."

"It's Henri Granville I'm thinking about, sitting in the middle of the Gironde Marshes not knowing that sometime after noon there'll be a knock at the door. I can see the smile on Jacaud's face now."

"And nothing we can do about it."

"Plenty, if we could get out of here. There's always the radio room in the tower, or the *Fleur de Lys* would be a better bet. A boat of that size is bound to have a radio telephone."

Guyon shook his head. "Those marshes are one of the most isolated places on the entire coast. Even if we managed to contact my people in Paris it would still be too late for Henri Granville. They'd never reach him in time."

"But we could," Mallory said. *"L'Alouette* will have to make the entire run submerged. That will take her a good three hours."

"It's almost an hour since she left," Guyon pointed out.

"Fleur de Lys has twice the speed. We could still beat Jacaud to the punch."

"Only if we get out of here within the next half-hour," Guyon said. "And I stopped believing in miracles a long time ago."

"We don't need a miracle. Just a little luck," Mallory pulled him down on the bed. "Now listen carefully."

It was cold in the passage and the young sailor shivered and got to his feet. He stamped vigorously to restore his circulation and walked a few paces away from the chair.

He was bored. He was also a little afraid. In the beginning the whole affair had seemed like a great adventure, a crusade. Now he was not so sure. He turned to move back to his chair and a muffled cry sounded from inside the cell.

He stood there, a puzzled frown on his face. There was another cry, followed by the crash of a bed going over. He arrived at the grille in time to see Guyon drive his fist into Mallory's face, knocking him against the wall.

"You got me into this, you bastard!" the young Frenchman cried. "I'll kill you! I'll kill you!"

He flung himself forward and Mallory ducked under another blow, moved in close and tripped him. A moment later and he was kneeling on Guyon's chest, hands twisted into his collar as he throttled him expertly.

The young sailor gave a cry of alarm. He pulled back the bolts and moved into the cell, revolver ready in his right hand. He reached for Mallory's collar and to his amazement Guyon erupted from the floor, grabbed his wrist savagely and twisted the revolver from his grasp. The sailor's mouth opened in a cry of alarm that was cut short as Mallory's fist moved in a short arc against the side of the jaw.

Mallory picked up the revolver, nodded to Guyon and they went outside quickly. All was quiet. Guyon bolted the door and they hurried along the passage.

A strange quiet reigned until they reached the main corridor when they heard voices in the distance and the clatter of pans from the kitchen. They passed along to the far end and Mallory opened the door cautiously and stepped on to the landing at the top of the steps which led down to the cave.

The jetty was deserted and *Fleur de Lys* and the speedboat were the only craft moored to the wall. They went down the stone steps quickly, paused for a moment at the bottom, then hurried across to *Fleur de Lys*.

When they went into the wheelhouse they saw at once that the radio telephone had been removed from its housing on the wall. Mallory grinned tightly. "He's a cautious bastard, I'll say that for him."

"Only to be expected." Guyon shrugged. "A good

soldier tries to foresee every eventuality." He looked around and shook his head. "This looks one hell of a size for two of us."

"We'll manage," Mallory said. "We'll have to. There's plenty of fuel in the tank, which is the main thing. Go get those lines off the jetty and we'll move out."

Guyon went forward quickly and untied the first line. As he started aft there was a harsh cry. When he glanced up he saw a sailor standing on the landing at the top of the steps. He ran along the deck and cast off the other line. The sailor drew a revolver and fired two wild shots as he came down the steps.

He was too late. The engines were already roaring into life and Mallory took *Fleur de Lys* out through the entrance. Spray splashed against the window, waves breaking over the deck as he turned through the lee-side of the reef and set course for Pointe du Château.

14

●

Force of Arms

HAMISH Grant opened the door and stood listening to the sound of quiet breathing. Fiona was stretched on the sofa and Anne slept in the wing-backed chair, a rug over her legs.

As he started to close the door she opened her eyes and said softly, "What time is it?"

"Just after eight. Jagbir's made some fresh tea."

She got to her feet, draped the rug over Fiona and followed him out. "Any sign of them?"

The old man shook his head. "Not yet."

The kitchen looked out over the courtyard, a large and pleasant room, beams supporting a low ceiling. Jagbir was frying eggs at the stove. When he saw Anne he poured a cup of tea and gave it to her and she stood in front of the fire, drinking it slowly.

Beyond, through the wide window, clouds hung threateningly over the fields, rain dripped from the gutters and brown leaves crawled across the cobbles. She went to the window and gazed out into the rain, thinking of Mallory.

Hamish Grant moved beside her and squeezed her hand.

147

"He did say it would take till breakfast-time. I shouldn'
worry too much if I were you."

"I'm not," she said. "One thing I *am* sure of is h
ability to look after himself, but I'd have thought we'
have heard from them by now."

"We very probably will before much longer."

She finished her tea and moved to the door. "I thin
I'll run down to the harbour and see what's happening."

"I'll send Jagbir with you."

She shook her head. "Let him get on with breakfast.
shan't be long. No need to wake Fiona till I get back. Sh
could do with the sleep."

She went along the hall, pulled on her sheepskin coa
and let herself out of the front door. Rain fell steadil
and she fastened a scarf about her hair as she went dow
the drive and turned through the gates.

Visibility was poor, a grey, clinging mist drifting i
patches across the water, and the central hill of the islan
looked very green against the leaden sky. She hurrie
along the road and paused on the brow of the hill to lool
down into the harbour. Only one boat was moored there
Raoul Guyon's launch, and the shooting brake was parke
at the end of the jetty.

She went down the hill quickly, taking a short cut acros
the wet grass. The shooting brake was beaded with mois
ture, the engine cold. She stood there for a moment, a
frown on her face, then walked along the jetty and steppe
on to the deck of Guyon's launch. She went into the smal
saloon, stood looking about her for a moment, then turne
to go.

She paused, wrinkling her nose, aware of the heavy
acrid taint of oil on the fresh morning air. It seeped into a
pool from under the door of the engine compartment. She
opened it and looked into a twisted mass of smashed
pipes and broken valves.

She crouched on one knee, gazing at the engine, her
mind frozen. As she started to rise, steps boomed hol-
lowly on the wooden planking of the jetty and Owen
Morgan called, "Hello below!"

Anne went up the companionway and came out on deck as he stepped down from the jetty. He wore an old blue pilot coat and rubber boots. Rain frosted his grey hair. He started to grin, but his smile faded at the sight of her troubled face.

"What's wrong?"

"Take a look at the engine."

He went down the companionway quickly. When he reappeared his face was grave. "Why would anyone want to do a thing like that?"

"To make sure we couldn't get off the island," she said.

He frowned quickly. "Look, how about letting me in on all this? Where's *Foxhunter?* I heard her go out early this morning."

"That must have been Colonel Mallory and Monsieur Guyon," she said. "They should have been back by now. I'm very much afraid something may have happened to them."

"Are they in some kind of trouble?"

"They could be, but there isn't time to explain now, Owen. We must get to Guernsey as soon as possible. What about your launch?"

"I hauled her up the slipway and into the boathouse ready for winter only two days ago," he said. "No trouble to bring her down again if it's all that urgent. I can have her ready for sea in half an hour."

"Do that," Anne said. "I'll go back to the house for the others. I'll explain things more fully when I get back."

She hurried along the jetty, climbed behind the wheel and switched on the engine. It required a lot of choke before it would turn over and Owen was already half-way up the slope towards the boathouse at the side of the hotel when she finally moved away.

The Welshman's skin crawled with excitement. Whatever was wrong, it was certainly serious. So much had been evident from Anne Grant's manner and actions, and to a man whose entire life had been a series of adventures the prospect of action carried all the kick of a good stiff drink. When he was only a few yards away from the boat-

house he remembered that the heavy door was padlocked
He turned and moved up the slope quickly to the sid
door of the hotel.

When he went into the kitchen Juliette was standin
at the sink washing the breakfast dishes. "Where's the ke
to the boathouse?" he demanded.

She turned, her eyebrows arching in surprise. "On th
nail behind the door where it always is. What's wrong?"

"I've got to get the boat out," he said. "The Grants wan
me to run them over to Guernsey. Can't explain why.
don't even know myself. But it must be something serious.'

He took down the key and went out again. After he had
gone Juliette Vincente stood at the sink, gazing blankly a
the door. After a moment she dried her hands carefully
hung up the towel and went up the back stairs to he
bedroom.

Owen Morgan opened the heavy doors of the boathous
and moved inside. The launch was seated firmly into a
deep concrete slot, a steel cable coiled around a winch a
her stern, holding her in place.

He jumped down on to the deck, pulled off the top o
the engine housing and paused suddenly, his throat goin
dry. The engine was in exactly the same state as the on
in Guyon's boat. Delicate pipes and valves smashed be
yond repair, a heavy hammer from his own tool-kit lying
in the ruins.

As he got to his feet there was the scrape of a shoe on
stone behind him. He turned and looked up at Juliette.
She wore his old corduroy jacket against the cold, her
hands thrust deep into the pockets.

"What's wrong, Owen?" she asked.

And then in one single, inexplicable flash of intuition he
knew that she was responsible and his eyes widened. "Why,
Juliette?" he said. "Why did you do it?"

"My brother was killed in Algeria, Owen." Her voice
was flat, lifeless. "He died for France. They repaid him by
giving what he'd died for away. I couldn't stand by and
allow that to happen."

Anger flared inside him like flames through dry leaves. "What sort of bloody nonsense are you telling me, girl? What about my boat?"

He started to clamber up beside her and she backed away, taking a revolver from her pocket. He stood facing her, very still, the skin on his face so white that it was almost transparent, a bewildered expression on his face.

"It's me, Juliette. Owen." He took a step forward.

"Move past me very slowly, Owen," she said. "Your hands behind your back. Don't make me kill you."

He stood poised, feet apart, and wild laughter erupted from his mouth. "Kill me, girl? You?"

In a moment he drove forward, one hand reaching for the gun, the other grabbing for her coat. In that same instant something seemed to move in her eyes and he knew with the most appalling certainty that he had made the last mistake of his life.

The sound of the shot re-echoed deafeningly between the walls of the boathouse and the force of the bullet, smashing through his body, sent him staggering backwards. He swayed on the edge of the ramp, hands clutching at his stomach, the blood erupted from his mouth in a bright stream and he fell back on the deck.

Juliette Vincente moved to the edge of the ramp and looked down at him. He lay very still, his dark eyes fixed on a point a million miles beyond her. She put the revolver back into her pocket, went outside and started to close the heavy doors. When she turned, *Foxhunter* was just coming round the point into the harbour.

In the kitchen Hamish Grant sat at one end of the table, the remains of his breakfast before him, and listened gravely to what Anne had to tell him.

When she had finished he shook his head briefly. "No use trying to pretend things look good. They don't. But one thing *is* certain. There isn't much we can do on our own."

"Then Guernsey is our only hope?"

He nodded and got to his feet. "I think it would be

better if we all went. It never pays to take chances an~~d~~
things could get rather unhealthy."

Fiona came in from the hall carrying his old British
warm. "You'll need this on, Father. It's rather cold."

It was the first time she had called him anything bu~~t~~
General since she was quite small, and his heart went ou~~t~~
to her. He reached for her face, dimly seen, and patte~~d~~
her cheek.

"Not to worry, Fiona. We'll get things sorted out."

She held his hand tightly for a moment, then turned an~~d~~
led the way into the hall. Anne was already sitting behin~~d~~
the wheel of the brake, the engine ticking over. The Gen~~-~~
eral and Jagbir got into the rear, Fiona in the front, an~~d~~
Anne drove away quickly.

It was still raining heavily and she turned on the wipers
leaning forward, watching for pot-holes in the dirt road.
As the brake climbed to the crest of the hill she change~~d~~
to a lower gear, ready for the descent to the harbour. The~~y~~
went over the top of the rise, Fiona gave a cry of alarm
and Anne braked quickly.

De Beaumont, Marcel and three sailors stood in the
road, looking out towards the sea. About a quarter of a
mile offshore, and running strongly south-west towards the
French coast, was *Fleur de Lys*. Marcel had one arm outstretched as he pointed. He turned to speak to de Beaumont and saw the shooting brake.

As they fanned across the road, Anne slammed her
foot hard against the accelerator in a reflex action that
took the old brake forward in a surge of power. She saw
the mouths open in alarm, voiceless above the roaring of
the engine, and then they were scattering to either side.
The brake shot through and bounced down on the road,
swerving on the bend at the bottom, cutting across the
grass towards the jetty.

She braked hard and the vehicle slewed in a long,
breathtaking skid that for one awful moment seemed to be
taking them over the edge to the beach and the rocks below. They came to a stop, the front bumper lodged against
a boulder, and she opened the door and got out.

There was no sign of Owen Morgan or his launch and when she looked up at the boathouse the great doors were still closed. She turned and found the General scrambling out at the rear, helped by Jagbir. As the little Gurkha straightened, his coat fell open to show the ivory-and-silver hilt of his *kukri,* the curved blade in its leather sheath thrust into his waistband.

As Fiona came round from the other side there was a faint cry up on the hill. Anne looked up and saw de Beaumont and his men running towards them. One of them paused, raised his rifle and fired a warning shot that whined across the jetty into the water.

Hamish Grant turned quickly. "What about Owen?"

"No sign of him or the launch," Anne said. "But *Foxhunter*'s moored at the end of the jetty."

Any brief hope that they might be able to take over the launch before de Beaumont and his men arrived disappeared as a saïlor came out of the wheelhouse, looked towards them, then hurried back inside.

"We'd better get up to the hotel," Anne said.

They started up the hill, Fiona leading the way, Hamish Grant using his walking stick to help him. There was another cry from de Beaumont and the sailor who had been guarding *Foxhunter* rushed out on deck with a rifle and loosed off a quick shot which splintered the woodwork of one of the boathouse doors.

Anne could taste blood in her mouth and there was a pain in her chest. She took Hamish Grant's hand and scrambled on, her feet slipping on the wet turf, and then they were on to the terrace and moving into the porch.

Fiona flung open the door and led the way inside. The bar was quite empty, a small fire burning in the grate. The stillness was so complete that Anne could hear her heart pounding.

Hamish Grant leaned against a table, struggling for breath, and she called out: "Owen! Owen Morgan! Where are you?"

There was no footfall and yet a quiet voice said with startling suddenness from behind her, "He isn't here."

Anne turned quickly and looked into the calm face of

Juliette Vincente. "For God's sake, Juliette. Where is he? What's going on?"

"I think that perhaps you have come to the wrong place, madame." Juliette's hand came out of her pocket, holding the pistol. "And now we will all wait quietly for the Comte de Beaumont."

In the same moment Jagbir drove forward, the terrible Gurkha battle-cry bursting from his throat. His hand swung from under his coat, the razor-sharp blade of the *kukri* hissing softly through space.

Juliette Vincente pulled the trigger twice, bullets smashing into the little Gurkha's body, and then he was on top of her. As she fired again at close quarters the heavy blade swung down, half severing her neck. They fell together, Jagbir on top, the *kukri* as firmly clenched in his right hand in death as it had been in life.

As Fiona screamed, the door swung open. Hamish Grant turned, pulling the Webley from his pocket, thrusting it towards the dark formless shadow against the light that was de Beaumont.

Behind him the window shattered and the barrel of a rifle was rammed painfully into his back. "If the General is wise he will drop it," Marcel said.

Hamish Grant stood there, trapped in the moment of decision, and already it was too late. De Beaumont moved forward and pulled the Webley gently from his grasp.

"And now, old friend, perhaps you will be sensible?"

15

•

The *Fleur de Lys*

FLEUR DE LYS rolled her slim length into the wind, plunging over a wave as water broke across her prow. In the wheelhouse Mallory leaned over the chart table. Behind him the wheel clicked to one side eerily to compensate as the vessel veered to starboard, the automatic pilot in control.

The Admiralty charts he had found in the flat drawers underneath the table were very comprehensive. The one which covered the Pointe du Château coastline and the Gironde Marshes told him everything he needed to know.

The door of the saloon companionway swung open and Guyon appeared. He wore a yellow oilskin jacket and carried a large mug of coffee in each hand.

"How are we doing?"

Mallory checked his watch. "Almost noon. Not long now. We're doing about fifteen knots."

"I heard the weather forecast on the radio in the galley just before I came up," Guyon said. "It wasn't good. Winds increasing and fog indicated in the coastal area."

"We're running into it already."

Mallory drank some of his coffee and Guyon peered

155

through the window. In the distance the fog waited like a damp shroud and heavy grey skies dropped towards the sea. Already the waves were lifting into whitecaps in the north-west.

"How far would you saw we're behind *L'Alouette* now?" Guyon said.

Mallory shrugged. "Submerged, she only has half our speed. Allowing for the start she had, it's going to run things a little close."

He leaned over the chart again. "She'll have to surface inshore of Île de Yeu before moving into the main creek flowing out of the marshes."

"What depth is it there?"

Mallory traced its course with a pencil. "Four or five fathoms. *Strong tidal currents constantly changing. Not to be relied on.* I know what *that* means. One day there's a sandbank. The next, six fathoms of clear water. These tidal marshes are all the same."

"But we could get in with *Fleur de Lys?*"

"I think so. Probably not as far as the central island where the cottage is. It's marked on the chart. Half a mile in."

Guyon straightened and the inimitable wry grin twisted his mouth. "Things might get interesting, eh?"

"I think you could say that."

Gradually the mist enfolded them until they were running through a strange, enclosed world and Mallory took over the wheel and reduced speed to ten knots. About thirty minutes later they emerged into a patch of clear water and saw the coastline of Pointe du Château no more than half a mile to port.

As they approached, a string of rocks and small islands lifted out of the sea, running parallel to the coast, trailing away towards the great hog-back of the Île de Yeu, looming out of the mist in the distance.

Mallory called to Guyon to take over the wheel and went back to the chart. When he straightened, his eyes glittered strangely.

"I think we can save a little time here, but it means taking a chance. *L'Alouette* will have to use the inshore passage. She has no other choice. This side of Île de Yeu, there's another passage marked between the island and the reef. Three fathoms."

"We might take the bottom out of her," Guyon said.

Mallory shrugged. "It's de Beaumont's boat, not mine."

Guyon grinned tightly. "Then I suggest you take the wheel."

Mallory changed course a point and the young Frenchman went down the saloon companionway. When he returned he carried two lifejackets.

"When I was a child a gypsy woman told my mother I must always beware of water. Superstitious nonsense, of course, but unfortunately my Breton blood says otherwise. I'd hate to prove her right at this stage."

Mallory changed to the automatic pilot, slipped his arms through the straps of the lifejacket and took over the wheel again. They were running parallel with the islands now and *Fleur de Lys* rocked in the turbulence, waves slapping solidly against her hull.

Rain hammered against the window, cascading in a sheet which blurred the outlines of all solid objects, adding a strangely dreamlike quality to the whole scene. Île de Yeu was very close and he could see white water boiling in a frenzy across the jagged spine of the reef.

He swung the wheel hard to port. *Fleur de Lys* shuddered protestingly, a wave slammed against her hull and the deck tilted. Guyon was thrown across the wheelhouse and Mallory fell to one knee. The wheel started to spin, but already his hands were back in position. As he brought her head round she lurched forward towards the narrow band of clear water between the reef and the island.

He gave her everything the engines had to offer and the boat responded magnificently. The passage rushed towards them at a seemingly impossible speed and then they were into it, water crashing across great rocks on either side, white, curling fingers reaching out to enfold them.

All around, boulders were appearing and disappearing, waves foaming over them and Raoul Guyon hung on to the chart table, his face white.

Strange, swirling currents snatched at the rudder and

for one agonizing moment *Fleur de Lys* slewed to port. Mallory heaved on the wheel. There was a slight, audible shudder that ran through the entire craft as she slid across a sandbank, and then they were into clear water.

Fog rolled from the land in patches and they could smell the foetid odour of the marshes that was carried towards them on the offshore breeze. Mallory reduced speed and they moved in, the engines rumbling protestingly on a low note.

The marshes drifted out of the fog, dark and sinister, waiting to receive them, and overhead a long wavering skein of geese passed like wind-blown spirits of the dead. Long, narrow sandbanks lifted out of the water and, landward, miles of rough grass marsh, a maze of creeks, waterlogged mud and wavering barriers of reeds.

They turned the end of a long sandbar and the mouth of the creek opened before them. Guyon leaned forward with a cry of alarm. Squatting just inside the entrance like some land-blown whale was *L'Alouette,* her grey-black plates shining with moisture. Fenelon stood in the conning tower with Jacaud and below three sailors were fitting an outboard motor to the stern of a large rubber dinghy.

Mallory took *Fleur de Lys* forward in a surge of power, her bow wave cascading across the hull of the submarine, knocking one of the sailors into the water. There was a startled cry and as they passed there was no more than ten feet between them. Mallory was aware of the shocked dismay on Fenelon's face, of Jacaud frowning in disbelief, and then they were through and safe in the fog.

He reduced speed to five knots and opened the window. Fog was sucked in, sharp and cold, the taste of it bitter as death. He strained his eyes into the gloom, watching the reeds drift by. A few minutes later they slid gently to a halt with a slight jar.

Mallory quickly reversed the engines. For a moment nothing seemed to be happening and then quite suddenly *Fleur de Lys* slid backwards.

"That settles that," he said. "We obviously aren't going to get any further."

He cut the engines, went out on deck and climbed on

op of the wheelhouse. The reeds were very thick at this
oint, but to the left was a small lagoon, circular in shape
nd perhaps a hundred feet in diameter.

He pointed to it as Guyon scrambled up beside him.
Our one chance."

He jumped to the deck, went into the wheelhouse and
tarted the engines. As they rumbled into life he spun the
vheel and crashed the boat into the reeds as she gathered
peed.

For a moment they seemed an impenetrable barrier
nd then they slowly parted and *Fleur de Lys* passed
hrough into the lagoon. Mallory cut the engines and she
noved slowly to the far end and came to a halt, her prow
rounding gently against a sandbank.

"No time to waste," he said. "One of us stays with the
oat. The other goes for Granville and his wife."

"That had better be me," Guyon said. "We have mutual
icquaintances. I think he would trust me."

Mallory pulled the chart forward. "You'll do better by
;oing on foot and swimming the intervening channels."
Ie opened a drawer and produced a pocket compass.

"Keep due west and you can't miss the central island.
About a quarter of a mile away."

"Getting Granville back here might be difficult," Guyon
aid. "He's an old man."

"But used to these marshes. That's why he comes here,
emember. You'll have to make out the best way you can."
Mallory produced the revolver he had taken from the
oung sailor at the castle and held it out. "Not much, but
better than nothing."

Guyon pushed it into the pocket of his oilskin jacket
ind went out on deck quickly. He jumped from the prow
o the sandbank and plunged into the reeds.

Mallory lit a cigarette and stood on deck in the quiet
ain. Perhaps five minutes later he heard the sound of an
outboard motor passing along the main channel. It moved
nto the distance, muffled by the fog, and then there was
only silence.

As Guyon went through the reeds a curlew whistled

hauntingly somewhere to the left and wildfowl called a
they lifted from the water, disturbed by his passing. H
came out on higher ground, checked the compass and ra
forward, alone in a land of shining mudflats, lonely creek
and everywhere the reeds.

He came to the end of solid ground and waded acros
a narrow creek, his feet sinking into soft mud. He coul
taste the salt on his lips and it stung his eyes painfully, bu
he kept on moving, pushing through the reeds into th
grey shroud.

Gradually the ground became firmer again until he wa
able to run across sand and coarse marsh-grass. A fev
moments later he stood on the banks of a shallow lake an
the house loomed out of the fog on its island fifty yard
away.

The evil, scum-covered waters reached out to meet hin
as he moved forward, and he took out the revolver an
held it above his head. It was not likely that the wate
would affect it, but there was no point in taking chances

It was surprisingly easy going, the mud giving way to
hard sand, and he was soon moving up on to dry land
again. As he ran towards the single-storeyed house a nar
row wooden jetty loomed out of the fog and he pause
abruptly. No boat was moored there, not even a marsh
punt. He stood there, a frown on his face, considering the
fact, then turned and went towards the house.

He could smell woodsmoke and saw it lifting in a blue
tracer from the rough stone chimney. He went up rickety
wooden steps to the porch, opened the door and went in

The room was furnished simply but comfortably, loose
rugs scattered across the polished wooden floor. There
were several bookcases, all filled, a sofa and two easy
chairs in front of the fireplace.

Logs smouldered fitfully on the stone hearth, heavily
banked with ashes that they might not burn too quickly
They told Guyon all he needed to know. Henri Granville
and his wife were not there. But, then, they should have
always counted on that as a possibility.

Ornithology was the old man's great hobby. He had

even written a book on the subject. It was quite obvious that at this moment he and his wife were sitting in their boat somewhere among the reeds which covered so many square miles of the marshes, probably even in some bird-hide since dawn taking photos.

He moved outside and went down to the jetty. Faintly, through the mist, came the sound of an outboard motor. Jacaud and his men. For them the solution would be obvious. They would simply wait for Granville to put in an appearance. No need even to go looking for him.

There was only one answer to the problem and Guyon waded into the lake and pushed towards the other side. He moved up on to high ground and ran along the shore towards the sound of the motor.

In spite of the clammy cold of the marshes sweat trickled from Fenelon's armpits. Ever since that first moment of shock when *Fleur de Lys* had passed them in the mouth of the estuary he had felt sick and frightened. And then de Beaumont's message over the radio, the mind numbing as the operator decoded it.

The message was quite plain. Under the circumstances they were to return at once. But that hadn't been good enough for Jacaud. He had insisted on going on into the marsh and Fenelon had wilted under his cold fury.

The reeds lifted like pale ghosts on either hand, the only sound the steady rattle of the outboard motor. He sat in the stern at the tiller, two sailors in the centre wtih rifles. Jacaud sat on the edge of the rounded prow, his sub-machine-gun slung around his neck as he gazed into the fog like some great bird of prey.

He turned, his granite, brutal face running with moisture. "We must be almost there. Cut the motor. We'll start paddling."

"You're wasting your time, Jacaud," Guyon called gaily. "I beat you to it. By now Henri Granville and his wife are well on their way out of here."

As the dinghy drifted forward, a sandbank reached out from the reeds like a pointing finger. Guyon stood on a small hillock at the far end. His hand swung up and he fired twice. One of the sailors groaned and went over the side, still clutching his rifle.

Jacaud slipped the sub-machine-gun over his head. It came up in a long, stuttering burst of fire, slicing through the reeds. He was too late. Guyon had disappeared like a ghost into the fog. He laughed mockingly somewhere near at hand and then there was silence.

The remaining sailor leaned over the side to pull in his comrade. Jacaud turned and struck up his arm. "Leave him. We haven't time."

The sailor recoiled from the killing fury, the devil's face that confronted him. The curious thing was that when Jacaud spoke his voice was quite calm.

"Back to *L'Alouette* and give that motor everything it's got. Mallory's got to return to Île de Roc. He's no choice. His girl-friend's still there. If we're lucky we can catch them on their way out to sea."

To Mallory the rattle of gunfire in the distance was like a physical blow and he walked the deck in impotent fury, hoping desperately that whatever had gone wrong Guyon had been able to handle it. Perhaps ten minutes later he heard the sound of the outboard motor returning along the creek. He stood very still, one foot on the rail, listening as it passed downstream.

He clambered on top of the wheelhouse and looked towards the west, straining into the fog. It was a good fifteen minutes before he heard the sound of brent geese calling bitterly as they lifted from the reeds. As the beating of their wings subsided, he was aware of movement towards the left.

He took a chance, cupped his hands and called: "Raoul! Over here!"

A couple of minutes later Guyon emerged from the fog and stumbled across the sandbank. Mallory ran to the prow and hauled him on board. Guyon was soaked to the skin and bitterly cold, his face pale and drawn.

"Have they passed yet?"

Mallory nodded. "What happened?"

Guyon explained briefly, shivering repeatedly as the wind cut through his damp clothes. "What do we do now?"

"Get to hell out of here and fast," Mallory said. "Unless I'm very much mistaken Jacaud will wait for us at the estuary. If we can get down there fast enough we might stand a chance of getting out to sea before they're ready."

"And back to Île de Roc?"

"That's the general idea. You'd better go below. Find yourself some dry clothes and a drink. I'll get things moving up here."

He went into the wheelhouse and started the engines. When he put them into reverse *Fleur de Lys* parted easily from the soft mud and he swung the wheel hard over, bringing her prow round until she pointed towards the wall of reeds that barred them from the creek.

He took her forward with a burst of speed, repeating his earlier manœuvre. Once again it proved successful. The reeds parted protestingly and the boat burst into the creek. He turned the wheel to starboard and she swung round, grazing the mud of the opposite bank.

He took her downstream slowly, the engines a murmur in the rain. Guyon came up from the saloon wearing khaki slacks, rubber boots and a heavy white sweater with a turtle collar. In one hand he carried a bottle of brandy, in the other a tin mug.

"How do you feel?" Mallory said.

Guyon grinned and held up the brandy. "How would you expect? It's Courvoisier. Like some?"

"I certainly would."

Mallory took the brandy down in two quick gulps. As a warm glow started to seep through his entire body he took out the packet of Gauloise that Marcel had given them and threw them to Guyon.

"Better have one while the going's good. Things might get pretty warm within the next ten minutes."

He took one himself and opened the window of the wheelhouse. Rain kicked into his face and there was a slight wind blowing in from the sea across the marshes, lifting the fog into weird shapes.

Visibility was down to thirty or forty yards, but the

reeds were beginning to drop back and the channel widened perceptibly. The water lifted in long swelling ripples and waves kicked against the bottom of the boat. They were almost there now and as a curving sandbank appeared a few yards to port he cut the engines and the current carried them in. There was a slight shudder and they stopped.

"What's the idea?" Guyon asked.

"I'd like to know what the opposition are up to. You stay here. I shan't be long."

Mallory jumped to the sandbank, landing knee-deep in water, waded out and followed its length into the fog until he could no longer see *Fleur de Lys*. A few minutes later he stood at the end, water splashing in across the sand, and looked out towards Île de Yeu. There was no sign of *L'Alouette* and he turned and ran back the way he had come, splashing through the shallows as the tide began to lift over the sandbank.

Fleur de Lys was already swinging out into the deepening channel and he took Guyon's proffered hand and scrambled over the rail.

"Not a sign of them. As far as I'm concerned I'm going to give her everything she's got and head out to sea. They'll have to come up with something pretty good to stop us."

He went into the wheelhouse, started the engines and reversed into the channel. Visibility was becoming rather better as the fog lifted and *Fleur de Lys* roared down the centre of the channel, her bow wave surging across the water on either side.

The mouth of the estuary appeared, clear and open to the sea, and Mallory swung the wheel to port to negotiate the great sandbank fifty yards beyond the entrance. As they turned the point, the current pushing against them, they found *L'Alouette* waiting.

Jacaud was in the conning tower, a heavy machine-gun mounted on a swivel pin. The moment they came into view he started to fire. Bullets swept across the deck and Mallory ducked as glass shattered in the wheelhouse.

Guyon crouched in the doorway, resting the revolver

across one raised arm, trying for a steady shot, but it was impossible. As bullets hammered into their hull, Mallory spun the wheel and the young Frenchman lost his balance.

It was the fog which saved them, a long, solid bank rolling in across the reef before the wind, and it swallowed them in an instant. Guyon picked himself up and stood listening to the impotent chatter of the machine-gun as Jacaud continued to fire. After a while there was silence.

He turned to face Mallory, his breath easing out in a long sigh. "I'd say that called for another drink."

As they emerged from the fog-bank, Mallory took them out to sea, giving the engines full power. He turned with a grin. "Nothing wrong there, thank God."

Guyon went into the saloon and returned with the Courvoisier. "He's made one hell of a mess down there. Holes all over the place. I don't think de Beaumont will be pleased."

Mallory swallowed some of his brandy and lit a cigarette. "We'll find out about that soon enough."

Guyon went into the saloon and Mallory inhaled deeply on his cigarette with a conscious pleasure. Everything was going to be all right, he was certain of that. Sometimes one got these feelings. The wind had freshened even more and spray spattered against the shattered windows of the wheelhouse. He pulled down the helmsman's seat and sat.

Some time later Guyon came in with sandwiches and hot coffee and Mallory switched to the automatic pilot. "Want me to take over?" Guyon asked.

Mallory shook his head. "In these conditions it should only take us two hours at the most to get there."

It was perhaps half an hour later that he became aware that they were slowing perceptibly. His attempts to adjust the controls met with no success and he switched to automatic pilot and went below.

Guyon was lying on one of the saloon divans, his head on his hands, eyes closed. As Mallory entered, he opened them and sat up.

"What's wrong?"

"God knows," Mallory said, "but we're losing speed badly and she isn't answering to the wheel like she should."

The *Fleur de Lys* heeled to starboard and there was a great rushing of water beneath their feet. He dropped to one knee, pulled back the carpet and peered inside. When he looked up his face was grave.

"There must be two dozen bullet holes along the water-line. We're leaking like a sieve. No wonder the damned thing's slowed down."

They went on deck quickly and into the wheelhouse. The electric pump was housed in a cupboard in one corner and the condition of the doors, splintered by bullets, told him what he would find.

He surveyed the smashed and twisted metal briefly, then turned, his face grim. "You'll find a hand-pump aft of the main engine housing. Do the best you can with that. Stick it as long as you can and I'll spell you."

"I see," Raoul Guyon said. "Things look bad, eh?"

"Only if *L'Alouette* catches us in this condition," Mallory said grimly.

Guyon moved out along the deck without a word and a moment later Mallory became aware of the harsh, rhythmic clangour of the hand-pump. He looked out of the window at the brownish-white stream of water gushing across the deck, took over the wheel and waited for *Fleur de Lys* to lighten.

16

●

Sea Fury

WHEN Fenelon first caught sight of *Fleur de Lys* his mind froze, refusing to accept for the moment what he knew to be an impossibility. The graticules misted over, temporarily obscured by a wave, and he raised the periscope a little more.

Fleur de Lys jumped into view, her familiar lines quite unmistakable. He said quickly to the rating at his side: "Fetch Monsieur Jacaud here. Tell him to hurry."

Jacaud arrived a few moments later. "What's going on?"

"Take a look."

The big man gripped the handles of the periscope tightly and lowered his head. When he turned to look at Fenelon a muscle twitched in his right cheek.

"I wonder what went wrong?"

Fenelon shrugged. "Perhaps you damaged her engines with the machine-gun, or even holed her. Does it matter? Shall I surface? We should be able to board her with very little trouble."

Jacaud shook his head and something glowed in the cold eyes. "I've got a better idea. Remember the *Kontoro?*

You said that one torpedo was all it would take. Let's see what you can do."

Fenelon felt the blood surge to his temples and his heart pounded wildly. "My God, it's perfect! They won't even know what hit them."

"I don't mind that," Jacaud said, "as long as there's nothing left afterwards."

L'Alouette carried two twenty-one-inch torpedoes, both mounted in the bow. Fenelon took a deep breath, pulled himself together and started to issue firm, crisp orders.

"Enemy's bearing, one-two-five. Course, one-three-one. Speed, six knots. Range, one thousand five hundred."

These facts, fed into a complicated electrical device, provided the angle of deflection, enabling the torpedoes to be aimed the right distance ahead of the target so that both should arrive in the same place at the same time.

A moment later the petty officer called, "Deflection, one-three degrees right, sir."

Fenelon raised the periscope handles, his face pressed to the rubber eyepiece. "Stand by both tubes."

"Both tubes ready, sir."

Fenelon could feel the sweat trickling down his face and his heart seemed to leap inside him. So often he had heard of this moment, had it described to him by men who knew. But for him this was the first.

"Stand by to fire."

Fleur de Lys seemed to leap into focus, every line of her clear and clean. His hands tightened on the handles. "Fire one."

The submarine lurched as the missile shot away and the hydrophone operator reported, "Torpedo running."

"Fire two."

Again the submarine shuddered.

"Torpedo running."

Fenelon turned to Jacaud. "Care to watch?"

The big man pushed him roughly to one side and bent to the handles.

On board *Fleur de Lys*, Guyon still sweated at the pump and the boat ran on, the automatic pilot in control while Mallory stood on top of the wheelhouse and swept the sea with a pair of glasses.

That *L'Alouette* would catch up with them now was certain. They were making no more than six knots and barely holding back the water. Submerged, the submarine had three or four knots on them. They were well out of the main shipping lane, he knew that. Their only hope was the chance of an odd fishing boat putting in an appearance, hardly likely considering the weather.

He swung the glasses again in a wide arc and stiffened as something lifted out of the water to starboard. It was a periscope, the tell-tale bow wave giving it away, and then he saw the great, surging streak of foam boiling under the surface of the water as it ran towards them.

"Torpedo!" he cried, and jumped to the deck, losing his balance and rolling over. He picked himself up, scrambled into the wheelhouse and grabbed for the wheel. He spun it round desperately, and slowly she started to turn. Guyon appeared beside him, adding his weight, shoving the wheel over, and then a great swell, rolling in from the west, gave them the final push.

Mallory left Guyon at the wheel and rushed to the rail. He was just in time to see the wash of the torpedo passing to starboard. A few seconds later it was followed by the second.

In the submarine Jacaud gave a growl of rage, turned and grabbed Fenelon by the jacket. "You missed, damn you! You missed!"

"But that's impossible."

Fenelon bent to the periscope and Jacaud pulled him away. "From now on I'm giving the orders. Take her in close and surface. I'm going to finish Mr. Bloody Mallory off personally."

On the *Fleur de Lys* Mallory was back at the wheel and Guyon worked the pump furiously. But it was no good. The boat rolled heavily, waves breaking across her prow, the weight of the water inside holding her down.

L'Alouette had fired both her tubes and no additional

torpedoes were carried by Type XXIII submarines, Mallory knew that. He looked out of the window, watching the fog roll in again in patches. There was no other vessel in sight, and his heart sank. Under the circumstances Jacaud's next move seemed obvious.

Somehow there was still a shock of surprise as the sea boiled in a great cauldron no more than fifty yards away and *L'Alouette* broke through to the surface. Even as the water still spilled from her plates Jacaud appeared in the conning tower. A rating came up beside him and they started to mount the heavy machine-gun on its firing-pin.

Guyon stood in the doorway, the revolver ready in his right hand. "Now what?"

"I think that's obvious," Mallory said flatly. "If I'm going to go I'm taking him with me. It's been nice knowing you."

"And you, *mon colonel*." Raoul Guyon drew himself together as if on parade. "An honour, sir."

He moved along the deck to the prow and Mallory swung the wheel and brought *Fleur de Lys* into the wind. A moment later and she was bearing down on *L'Alouette*.

Jacaud started to fire, bullets hammering into the prow, and Mallory braced himself, hands firm on the wheel. Guyon lay flat on the deck, one arm around a stanchion, waiting for the moment of impact. There was two rounds left in the revolver and he was praying that at the last he might have the chance of putting them both into Jacaud.

In the conning tower of *L'Alouette* Jacaud still fired the machine-gun, raising it slightly, aiming for Mallory in the wheelhouse. Fenelon appeared beside him, his face white and terrified, mouth open in a soundless scream.

Mallory was aware of all these things, of the bullets hammering into the wheelhouse as he ducked out of sight and then *Fleur de Lys* was lifted high on a swell. She seemed to poise there for a moment, then slid down the other side into *L'Alouette,* her prow grinding against the side of the conning tower where it joined the hull.

There was a terrible crash, a groan of tortured metal as the bow crunched into the plates, cutting through the ballast tanks, crushing the pressure hull. *L'Alouette* heeled, the conning tower leaning over, spilling the machine-gun into the water, and Jacaud and Fenelon hung on desperately.

Guyon was on his feet, leaning over the rail. As he took aim and fired *Fleur de Lys* lurched to one side and he went head first into the sea.

Fleur de Lys kept on moving, her steel hull sliding over the submarine, pushing it down into the water. Suddenly she was across, her prow plunging into a wave. Mallory got to his feet, grabbed the wheel and struggled to bring her round.

Incredibly, she answered, and lifted sluggishly over the swell, her engines still beating. He turned and looked out through the shattered windows at the submarine.

She had righted herself now, but the sea was breaking over her hull in sinister fashion. The forward hatch opened and several sailors emerged. Jacaud came down the outside ladder to join them.

They were pointing at something in the sea and Mallory saw Raoul Guyon, a swell lifting him up and carrying him in towards the submarine. As he was washed across the grey hull they pounced on him.

There was nothing Mallory could do and he kept on going, passing into the fog. When he glanced back five minutes later *L'Alouette* was lost to view.

Gradually the engines lost power and progress became slower. The fog was very patchy, blown by a strengthening wind, and in the distance he could see Île de Roc low on the horizon. The engines stopped altogether, five minutes later, with a hiss of steam.

He went down into the flooded saloon, found the bottle of Courvoisier and went back on deck. The fog had cleared even more now, but the wind was cold and the waves were lifting again.

He unshipped the dinghy and waited until the green waters started to slop across the deck, then he slid it over the stern and climbed in. He rowed away, paused and watched *Fleur de Lys* slide under the surface.

The water boiled for a little while, then calmed into a great white patch of froth, a coil of rope, a box and one or two loose spars floating in the centre. It was always a saddening sight, the loss of a good ship. He inflated his lifejacket, raised the bottle of Courvoisier to his lips and started to row.

L'Alouette drifted low in the water, her powerful diesels still working, pushing her towards the island. Progress was agonizingly slow and in the conning tower Jacaud waited, a cigarette in his mouth, watching the island grow nearer in the gathering dusk.

Below, things were bad and getting worse every minute. The crew worked knee-deep in water and it took the petty officer all his time to keep them under control.

Fenelon lay on the bunk in his tiny cabin, lips moving soundlessly as he stared up at the bulkhead. He shivered as if he had the ague and when someone attempted to speak to him he gazed at the man with vacant eyes.

Guyon lay huddled in a corner of the conning-tower bridge, blood oozing from a nasty gash in his forehead, knocked insensible by Jacaud the moment they had hauled him from the sea.

Jacaud stirred him with his boot, wondering exactly how he was going to kill him. It would have been easy to leave him in the sea or even to put a bullet through his head the moment they hauled him aboard, but that would have been too simple. Guyon deserved something special. He was a traitor and had been all along the line.

The throb of the diesels faltered and stopped and in the silence which followed there was a startled cry from inside the submarine. The forward hatch opened and the crew poured out. They brought with them several inflatable dinghies, including the one with the outboard motor which Jacaud had used in the marshes.

Jacaud picked Guyon up, slung him over one shoulder with easy strength and went down the ladder. He walked along the hull and paused a couple of yards away from the frightened sailors. They were no more than a quarter of a mile from the great reef which linked Île de Roc and St. Pierre, the tide carrying them in. Jacaud did not intend to wait and see what happened to *L'Alouette* when she was pounded across those terrible rocks.

He nodded to the petty officer. "I'm taking the one with the outboard motor. You're coming with me."

There was a chorus of startled cries from the men and one of them rushed forward. "Why you? Why not us?"

Jacaud took a Lüger from his pocket and shot the man twice in the chest, the bullets knocking him into the water. There was a sudden silence and they all crowded back.

A few moments later the largest dinghy was moving away, the petty officer in the stern operating the outboard motor. Jacaud sat in the prow facing him and Guyon sprawled in the bottom.

The power of the current was already swinging the doomed submarine in towards the reef and there was a confused shouting on deck. One by one, the men crowded into the remaining dinghies and the current immediately swept them away.

Below in *L'Alouette* Fenelon lay in his cabin, forgotten by everyone. It was only when the water reached his bunk that he came to his senses. He sat up, stared down at it for a moment, then suddenly seemed to come to life.

He moved outside and started forward. At that moment the lights went out. He screamed as darkness enfolded him and started to feel his way along desperately.

As he reached the control room, light streaming in through the open conning tower, water started to cascade down the ladder and the whole world seemed to turn upside down.

He was aware of the crash, the rending of the metal plates and then a green cascade mercifully engulfed him. The sea swung *L'Alouette* in across the reef. For a brief moment she poised on the edge, then plunged down into the darkness of the Middle Passage.

17

•

The Run to the Island

THE oars dipped and rose and Mallory pulled with all his strength, but his arms were tired and already there was a blister in one palm from a splinter in the rough handles.

It was more than an hour since *Fleur de Lys* had gone down and he had rowed steadily for most of that time, making little progress. The fog still hung low over the water in long, wraithlike patches. On one occasion he seemed to hear a faint cry. When he looked back there was a brief flash of yellow on top of a wave as one of the submarine's rubber dinghies was swept out to sea.

After a while he stopped and rested on the oars. Île de Roc was still half a mile away and it was quite obvious that the run of the tide was sweeping him on a parallel course with the island that would eventually take him out to sea.

Even if he fetched up in the steamer lane that ran up-Channel from Ushant it would be dark in another hour. He was under no illusions about his ability to survive a night in the Channel in such a frail craft.

There were two good doubles left in the bottle of Courvoisier. He took them down slowly and tossed the empty bottle into the sea. As a thin rain drifted down on the wind he reached for the oars and started to row again.

The freshening wind dispelled the last traces of fog and an ugly chop formed on the water. He pulled steadily, staring into the gathering twilight, his mind a blank, everything he had of brain and muscle concentrated on his impossible task.

When he paused twenty minutes later and looked over his shoulder he saw to his astonishment that he was now quite close to the island. There was a slapping sound against the keel of the dinghy and it swung round, swirling past a long finger of rock, moving in fast, caught by some inshore current.

He bent to the oars with renewed vigour, forgetting the pain in his right hand, the blood that dripped steadily down. The current helped, carrying him closer inshore every minute. The waves were higher now as they pounded in over the rocks and water started to slop across the dinghy's stern.

He heaved on the oars, trying to keep her head round, but it was too much for him. He let them go, knelt in the bottom and waited, holding on with both hands.

The cliffs were very close now, the surf white as it crashed in across the narrow beach, breaking over ledges of rock. Behind Mallory a great, heaving swell rolled in, gathering momentum, sweeping him in before it. A sudden rending crash jarred his spine. Water foamed around, spray lifting high into the air. The dinghy ground forward across jagged rocks, her boards splintering, and came to a halt, the prow wedged into a crevasse.

Mallory hung on, and as the sea receded with a great sucking noise he scrambled out of the dinghy and stumbled across the final line of rocks. A moment later he was safe on the strip of beach at the base of the cliffs.

He sat down, holding his head in his hands, and the world spun away. The taste of the sea was in his throat and he retched, bringing up a quantity of salt-water.

After a while he got to his feet and turned to examine the cliffs behind. They were no more than seventy or eighty feet high and sloped gently backwards, cracked and fissured by great gullies.

It was an easy enough climb and he scrambled over the edge a few minutes later and turned to look out to sea. The fog had disappeared completely now, but darkness was falling fast and the moon was already rising above the horizon.

He hurried through the wet grass, following the slope in a gentle curve that brought him over the edge of the hill ten minutes later on the far side of the harbour from the Grants' house.

The cove looked strangely deserted, no smoke rising from the chimney of the hotel. He was aware of Guyon's launch, of the shooting brake tilted against a rock, the long skid-marks trailing back up the grassy slope to the road. He went down the slope on the run.

He walked round to the front of the hotel, calling loudly without receiving any reply. When he opened the door and stepped into the bar he was already prepared for something out of the ordinary, some evidence of a struggle at least.

Jagbir and Juliette Vincente still crouched together by the bar, a pool of dried blood spreading into the rush matting.

It was very quiet, too quiet, and for a moment Mallory seemed to hear the sea roaring in his ears and there was an element of unreality to it all. It was as if none of this were really happening, and he turned and stumbled outside.

He wasted five minutes in going down to the jetty in the forlorn hope that Guyon's launch might be seaworthy. It was almost completely dark when he breasted the hill and trotted towards the Grants' house.

He went in through the kitchen and quiet enveloped him, that strange, secret stillness a house wraps about itself when no one is there, and an overwhelming loneliness surged through him.

He spoke aloud, his voice hoarse and broken: "Anne?"

But only the house listened to him and the quiet ones. He stumbled into the sitting-room, opened the cabinet and poured himself a brandy. He stood there, sipping it quietly remembering her here by the fireside in the soft lamplight a thousand years ago.

The darkness seemed to move in on him with a strange whispering, and he closed his eyes tightly, fighting the panic, the despair which rose inside him. The moment passed. He put down the glass and went out through the french windows.

The moon was clear and very bright, stars strung away to the horizon. When he topped the hill on the western side of the island St. Pierre and the castle were etched out of black cardboard, breathtakingly beautiful like something from a child's fairy-tale.

Beneath him the tide was already on the turn, white water breaking across the great reef, rocks thrusting their heads into the moonlight. Minute by minute the water would continue to drop until for one brief hour a jagged causeway linked the two islands. One hour only and then the tide would come roaring in. But there was no point in thinking about that. Such had been his haste since landing from the dinghy that he had not even had time to rid himself of his lifejacket. He touched it mechanically, moved along the cliffs till he came to a sloping ravine that slanted to the beach below, and started down.

Marcel unbolted the heavy door and de Beaumont moved inside. There was no window, but the room was brightly illuminated by a naked bulb which hung from the centre of the low ceiling. Guyon and Hamish Grant sat on a couple of old packing cases, talking in low tones.

They came to their feet, the old man leaning on his walking stick. Guyon was very pale, dark circles under his eyes, and the gash on his forehead was red and angry.

"It seems I must congratulate you, Captain Guyon," de Beaumont said calmly.

Guyon shook his head. "No need. You were doomed from the beginning. A pity you didn't realize that a few lives ago."

"I wouldn't be too sure. The game isn't over yet."

"It will be the moment Colonel Mallory makes land."

"And what if he doesn't? From what I hear, *Fleur de Lys* was in a sinking condition when last seen."

"You're forgetting Granville and his wife. They must have contacted the authorities now. The sands are running out, de Beaumont. You were wrong from the start, always have been. We don't need you and your bully-boys to tell us how to govern France."

Marcel took a step forward and de Beaumont pushed him back. "Let him go on."

"A country's greatness lies in the hearts of her people, not in the size of her possessions, and France is people. In one way or another, blood and suffering is all they've been given since 1939 and they've had enough. But not you, Colonel. You couldn't stop if you wanted to."

"Anything I have done I have done to the greater glory of France," de Beaumont said.

"Or the greater glory of Philippe de Beaumont? Which is it? Can you tell the difference? Have you ever been able to?"

De Beaumont's face seemed to sag, and for the first time since Guyon had known him he looked like an old man. He turned and walked out. Marcel hesitated and then followed him. The door closed and the bolts rasped into place.

"Quite a speech," Hamish Grant said out of the long silence which followed.

"Accomplishing precisely nothing," Guyon said wearily, and sat down, his head in his hands.

"Worth hearing, though." The old man patted him gently on the shoulder, resumed his seat and they waited.

De Beaumont stood in front of the great glass window of the tower room and looked out over the sea. Far, far to the west the rim of the ocean was tipped with orange fire, Île de Roc dark against the sky.

The beauty of it was too much for a man and he opened the casement and inhaled the good salt air and out beyond the island the lights of a ship seemed very far away.

Life was a series of beginnings and endings, that much at least he had learned. He remembered Dien-Bien-Phu,

standing on the edge of a foxhole in the rain as the tricolour was hauled down and little yellow peasants from
the rice fields had swarmed over the broken ground to
take him and what was left of his men.

And then Algeria. Years of bloodshed. Of death in the
streets and death in the hills. He had believed implicitly
that the end justified the means, but what if that end was
never realized? What if one were left only with the blood
on the hands? Blood which had been shed to no purpose,
which could never be washed off.

He felt curiously sad and drained of all emotion. A
small wind moaned around the tower and then there was
only the silence. In that single moment the heart turned
to ashes inside him. Looking out over the moonlit sea he
knew with a bitter certainty that he had been wrong. That
in the final analysis all that he had done came to nothing.
That everything Raoul Guyon had said was true.

He walked to the fireplace and looked up at the old
battle standard for a long moment. He nodded, as if coming to some secret, hidden decision.

He picked up the telephone and pressed an extension
button. When the receiver was lifted at the other end he
said briefly, "Send up Jacaud."

He replaced the phone, moved across to a narrow door,
opened it and stepped into the small turret bedroom. Anne
Grant sat in a chair by the window. Fiona lay on the bed.

They got to their feet and faced him. He bowed courte-
ously and stood to one side. "If you would be so kind."

They hesitated perceptibly, then brushed past him. He
closed the door, moved to the fire and turned.

"What have you done with my father?" Fiona demanded.

"There is no need to alarm yourself. He will come to no
harm. I give you my word."

"And Raoul Guyon?"

De Beaumont smiled faintly. "A great deal has taken
place of which you are not aware. Captain Guyon is at
this moment with General Grant. Except for a nasty cut on
the head he seemed in fair condition when I saw him an
hour ago."

"You haven't mentioned Colonel Mallory," Anne said carefully.

De Beaumont shrugged. "All I can say with truth, my dear, is that at this precise moment I haven't the slightest idea where he is."

There was a knock at the door, it opened and Jacaud entered. He came forward and waited, the cold eyes in the brutal, animal face giving nothing away.

"Have *Foxhunter* refuelled and made ready for sea," de Beaumont said.

"I've already seen to it. Are we leaving?"

"I should imagine it would be the sensible thing to do. Even if Mallory hasn't managed a landfall yet Granville must certainly be in touch with the French authorities by now. Admittedly they will then have to contact British Intelligence, but I shouldn't imagine it will be long before we're faced with some sort of official delegation."

"Where are we going—Portugal?"

"Perhaps you, but not me, Jacaud." Philippe de Beaumont extracted a cigarette from his case and fitted it carefully into his holder. "We leave in half an hour for Jersey. When you have landed me in St. Helier you are a free man. You and the others may go where you please."

Jacaud's eyes narrowed. "Jersey? Why would you want to go there?"

"Because they possess a more than adequate airport, my dear Jacaud, and an early-morning flight to Paris. I intend to be on it."

"You must be mad. You couldn't walk ten yards along the Champs Élysées without somebody recognizing you."

"No need," de Beaumont said calmly. "You see, I intend to place myself in the hands of the authorities."

For once Jacaud's iron composure was shattered. "Give yourself up? You'd face certain execution."

"That would be for the court to decide." De Beaumont shook his head. "I've been wrong, Jacaud. We all have. I thought I wanted what was best for France. I see now that what I really wanted was what was best for me. Further bloodshed and violence would accomplish nothing. The events of the past few days have taught me that."

"And what about the women and the old man? What do we do with them?"

"We can release them before we leave. They'll be picked up before long."

"And Guyon?"

"Him we will also leave."

Rage erupted from Jacaud's mouth in a growl of anger. "I'll see that one on his back if it's the last thing I do on top of earth. God in heaven, I could have left him to drown."

"Sergeant-Major Jacaud!" De Beaumont's voice was like cold steel. "I have given you certain orders. You will see that they are carried out. Understand?"

For a dangerous moment the fire glimmered in Jacaud's eyes, and then, quite suddenly, he subsided. "I beg the Colonel's pardon."

"Accepted. Release Captain Guyon and General Grant and bring them up here. We leave in half an hour."

Jacaud opened the door and went out. De Beaumont sighed, and said almost to himself: "Twenty-three years of blood and war. Too much for any man."

It was Anne who answered him, her face very pale. "Before God, Colonel de Beaumont, I pity you."

He took her hand and kissed it gently, then crossed to the door to the turret room and opened it. "Perhaps you would wait in here?"

They walked past him. He closed the door and went to the fireplace. He looked up at the standard for a long moment, then sat down at his writing desk and picked up a pen.

Marcel sat at the table in his tiny room, a bottle of cognac in front of him. He was reading an old magazine, turning the pages slowly, his mind elsewhere. They should have been out of this place the moment Jacaud had returned with the news of the loss of *L'Alouette,* so much was obvious. He wondered what de Beaumont had wanted, and raised his glass to his lips. Behind him the door crashed open and Jacaud entered.

His face was white, the skin drawn tightly over the

prominent cheekbones, and there was a strange, smoky look in his eyes that made Marcel's flesh crawl.

"What is it? What happened up there?"

Jacaud grabbed the glass, filled it with cognac and swallowed it down. "He wants us to take him to Jersey. From there he intends to fly to Paris to hand himself over to the authorities."

"He must be mad." Marcel's face turned a sickly yellow colour. "Are you going to let him?"

"Am I hell. If they get him they get all of us. It would only be a matter of time."

"What about the prisoners?"

"He's going to release them."

Marcel jumped up in alarm. "We've got to get out of here. This whole thing's going sour."

"We're getting out of here all right, but on our own," Jacaud said. "Just you and me. Everyone else can go to the devil. But first I've got to settle with de Beaumont. He knows too much for his own good."

"And Guyon?"

"I'll have to forgo that pleasure. You take care of him and the old man. I'll see you on the jetty in fifteen minutes."

He went out and Marcel raised the bottle of cognac to his lips, swallowed deeply and tossed it into a corner.

It was quiet in the corridor and he moved quickly along to the end and paused outside a stout wooden door. He took a revolver from his pocket and checked it quickly. There were four rounds in the cylinder and he unbolted the door, kicked it open and moved inside.

Raoul Guyon and General Grant rose to meet him. Marcel closed the door behind him and moved forward.

"You first, Captain," he said, and his hand swung up.

Guyon flung himself to one side and the bullet chipped stone from the wall. In the same moment Hamish Grant slashed at the light with his walking stick, plunging the room into darkness.

Marcel cried out sharply and fired twice. He was aware of a shadow moving over towards the right in the split-

second flash and fired twice again. The second time the
hammer clicked on an empty chamber. He flung the use-
less weapon into the darkness with a sob and reached for
the door.

There was the scrape of a foot behind him and a great
arm slid around his neck. He was aware of the pain, of the
relentless brute strength, and struggled wildly. Hamish
Grant increased the pressure, his fingers locked together
like steel bands, and the Frenchman went limp.

The old man dropped him to the floor and said hoarsely,
"Raoul, where are you?"

There was a movement in the darkness beside him.
"Here, General."

Hamish Grant put out a hand and touched him on the
shoulder. "Are you hit?"

"Not a chance," Guyon said. "But let's get out of here.
We must find the girls."

The old man opened the door cautiously and walked
into the passage. Something moved, a dark shadow
against the light. He reached out, a snarl rising in his
throat, and his wrists were gripped tightly.

A tired, familiar voice said: "All right, General. It's
me."

18

●

Last Round

MALLORY struggled across a great slippery mass o
rounded stones and paused on top of a natural escarp
ment. He had never felt greater loneliness in his entir
life. On each side stretched the sea, and before him, clea
in the moonlight, the sinister, twisted maze of jagged rock
and great boulders that made up the reef.

At high water the escarpment upon which he was nov
standing would be a good five fathoms deep, and he
moved on, slipping and stumbling across a morass o
slimy seaweed, sinking up to his knees in places.

It had taken him three-quarters of an hour to get half
way along the reef. With each passing moment it became
more and more apparent that unless he could increase hi.
rate of progress the tide would sweep back in to pound
him across these cruel rocks.

He came out on to a strip of wet sand shining in the
moonlight, and started to run. For perhaps a hundred
yards the sand held true and then petered out into grave.
and broken stone.

He entered a forest of dark pointing fingers which
lifted into the moonlight like some strange prehistoric

monument and wasted ten minutes finding his way
through. As he struggled out along a shelving bank of
seaweed he paused and looked down at moonlight shining
on the waters of the Middle Passage.

It stretched before him, a dark tunnel with at least
twenty feet of headroom at low water. The wind blowing in from the sea, scattering spray in his face, decided
him. At his present rate of progress he was certain to be
caught. There was only one remaining chance of beating
the tide and he slid over the edge.

Strangely enough, when he entered the water he wasn't
aware of the cold and his lifejacket worked perfectly. He
turned on to his back and started to swim, using both
arms in a powerful back stroke.

The passage was shadowy in the moonlight and very
still and the sound of the sea outside seemed to come from
another place. He remembered what lay beneath him,
fathoms deep in the darkness, and pushed the thought
away, concentrating all his strength on the task in hand.

It was perhaps fifteen minutes later that he became
aware of a different note outside and spray foamed through
the crannies above his head, splashing across his face.
The water-level started to rise at once and with every
passing minute the roof came nearer.

He turned on his face and swam forward, thrashing
wildly with his feet. A few moments later he came out into
a jagged basin. As a swell lifted him up he grabbed for a
ledge and hauled himself out of the water.

The tide was already moving in, licking hungrily at the
rocks, and far out to sea a flash of sheet lightning illuminated the sky. He came to the end of the main body of the
reef and before him a long, thin spine of rock and gravel
stretched three hundred yards to St. Pierre.

He started to run, aware of the roaring of the sea,
hungry for him as she swept in to drown the land, erupting with phosphorescence, blue-green lights dancing on
the water, dissolving as rapidly as they appeared.

To the right, lightning flared again and a dark band of
shadow moved across the sky, snuffing out the stars. He
came to a long strip of shingle and started to run.

Half-way across, the sea splashed in knee-deep. He struggled forward, aware of its strength as it tugged at him. It was already at his waist when he reached the sprawling mass of boulders heaped at the base of the island. As his feet missed bottom, he thrashed forward, grabbed for a ledge and hauled himself out.

Still the sea rose, and he moved on, aware only of the menace behind. He skirted the base of the cliffs and finally reached a point of jagged rock no more than twenty feet from the entrance to the cave.

He jumped into the water and started to swim desperately, but there was no need. The tide swept him into the entrance on the crest of a great swell. A moment later he bumped against the wall of the jetty at *Foxhunter*'s stern. He swam round to a flight of stone steps and climbed out of the water.

He was tired, more tired than he had ever been in his life, and the roaring of the sea seemed to have got inside his head. He pulled off his lifejacket, padded across the jetty and went up the steps, keeping to the wall. When he reached the landing all was quiet. He opened the door cautiously and moved forward.

There were three doors on this section of the corridor, all leading to rooms used as quarters by *L'Alouette*'s crew. He searched them quickly, hoping for a weapon, but found nothing.

As he emerged from the last he heard the muffled reports of several gunshots fired close at hand. He stood listening intently. Another shot sounded. He went along the passage, every sense alert, and paused at the end.

Behind him a door opened. He whirled round, hands coming up, and Hamish Grant stepped into the light.

The great hall was a place of shadows. No fire burned in the hearth and a single light at the far end gave the only illumination. Mallory moved out of the doorway and stood listening, but there was no sound, and he moved forward followed by Guyon and Hamish Grant.

There was a small lamp bracketed to the wall of the gallery and for some reason it seemed to grow dimmer as he went upstairs. He paused, swaying a little, and Guyon's anxious voice seemed to come from a great distance.

"Are you all right?"

Mallory opened his eyes, nodded and moved on, putting one foot in front of the other mechanically. It was only when they reached the door to the tower and he pushed it open that he realized how exhausted he was. There was no strength left in him at all.

Guyon and the old man crowded into the narrow hall and Mallory bolted the door. "Whatever happens now, no one else gets in," he said, and the words seemed to be spoken by someone else.

He took a deep breath, summoning together every final resource of body and mind, and led the way up the stairs. The walls spiralled round, the night sky gleaming through the slotted windows, and somewhere thunder rumbled menacingly.

When they emerged on the first landing the door to the radio room stood open and there was no one there. Mallory moved across to the set and switched it on. There was a faint crackling of static. He picked up the microphone and high in the tower three shots were fired in rapid succession. A moment later Fiona Grant screamed.

Jacaud paused on the landing, took the Lüger from the pocket of his reefer coat and removed the clip. It was by no means full, he could tell that by the weight, but there was no time to reload. He slammed it back into the butt, replaced the Lüger in his pocket and opened the door.

De Beaumont was sitting at his desk writing, his hair silver in the soft light. He blotted the sheet of paper carefully, put down his pen and looked up.

A frown appeared on his face. "What's happened, Jacaud? Where are General Grant and Guyon?"

"Marcel is taking care of them now," Jacaud said calmly.

"Taking care of them? I don't understand."

"Don't you, my brave colonel?" Jacaud laughed harshly. "Did you really think I'd stand to one side and allow you to fly off to Paris to play *le grand seigneur,* a de Beaumont to the end?"

"How dare you!" de Beaumont said hoarsely.

"For you it's always been a game," Jacaud said. "A great and wonderful game with bugles blowing and standards flying in the breeze like some medieval set-piece. That's the way you've lived and that's the way you want to die, but not this time, Colonel. They'll squeeze you so hard you'll tell them everything that's ever happened to you since you were three years old. Unfortunately for you, that includes me."

De Beaumont grabbed a glass paperweight, hurled it with all his force and reached for the handle of the drawer containing his revolver. Jacaud jumped to one side, the paperweight smashing against the wall, and fired.

The bullet caught de Beaumont in the left shoulder, spinning him round, and Jacaud fired again twice, the impact driving de Beaumont forward. He clutched at the mantelpiece, the linen material of his jacket bursting into flames, and reached up towards the old battle standard. He started to fall, his fingers catching at the fringe, and it fluttered down to cover him like a scarlet shroud.

The door of the turret room opened and Anne and Fiona Grant appeared. The young girl screamed once, her hands going up to her face. Jacaud ignored them. He walked slowly across the room and stood looking down at de Beaumont, a dazed expression in his eyes.

Behind him the door swung open with a crash. As he turned, Raoul Guyon hurled himself forward. Jacaud's first bullet chipped the wall beside the door, his second caught Guyon just above the left breast, stopping him in his tracks. Guyon groaned and fell to one knee. Jacaud raised the Lüger, took careful aim and fired again.

As the hammer fell on an empty chamber, Anne Grant flung herself forward, grabbing at his arm. He hit her backhanded, slamming her against the wall, and reached into his pocket for some spare rounds.

Mallory seemed to fill the doorway, the eyes dark shadows in a face that was lined with fatigue. He started forward, swaying slightly from side to side, eyes never leaving Jacaud, no expression on his face, a dead man walking.

Jacaud dropped the Lüger, seized the heavy brass poker from the fireplace and weighed it in his hand, a savage smile on his face.

"Come on!" he said. "Come on, you bastard!"

Mallory stood there, hands hanging loosely at his sides, fatigue washing over his face, and Jacaud sprang forward, the brass poker swinging down, gleaming in the lamplight.

To Mallory that blow was like a branch swaying in the wind. As the poker came down he grabbed for the wrist, twisting the arm up and out to one side, taut as a steel bar, using the same terrible grip he had used on the jetty at Southampton so long ago.

Jacaud screamed, dropping the poker, and the muscles of his shoulder started to tear. Mallory reached for the wrist with his other hand and twisted it round and up.

Again there was a tearing sound as muscle gave and Jacaud screamed again. Still keeping that terrible hold in position, Mallory ran him head first across the room towards the great window. It dissolved in a snowstorm of flying glass and Jacaud dived into darkness, his last cry swept away on the wind like some departing spirit.

Raoul Guyon was propped against Fiona's knee, his face hollow with pain, and Hamish Grant stood in the doorway. When Mallory turned, blood on his face from the flying glass, they were all looking towards him strangely.

He started to fall and strong arms caught him, easing him down to the floor, and he looked up at Anne Grant, that dark, dear face so full of love for him.

"Raoul?" he said. "How's Raoul? Is it serious?"

"He's going to be fine."

There was something else, something important. He frowned desperately and then remembered. "The radio room—downstairs. We must call Jersey. There are three motor torpedo boats just waiting for the right signal."

"It's all right," she said. "Everything's all right. We'll take care of it."

She pillowed his head against her breast, her arms about him. He turned into their softness, the sound of the sea in his ears, and slept.

ABOUT THE AUTHOR

JACK HIGGINS was born in Belfast, and grew up in Northern Ireland and in Yorkshire, England. After spending three years in the Horse Guards, he worked for degrees in sociology and social psychology. Higgins is the author of more than twenty-five novels, including *The Keys of Hell, The Savage Day, The Eagle Has Landed,* and *Storm Warning.*